JOSEPH COVINO JR

FRANCESCO FERRARI
EXPLORES
CHINATOWN

EPIC PRESS

DEDICATION

FOR
SHIH-TSENG CHUANG
(1955–2013)
AND
HER EVER BLESSED
MEMORY

If you could
See my smiles
In blossom flowers;
Hear my whispering
In singing birds, My Beloved,
You'll see a golden unicorn
In your dream…
One moonlight in Spring.
If you would,
If you love me.
—Shih–Tseng Chuang, 10 June 1985

CONTENTS:

PROLOGUE: *DOWN AND OUT IN CHINATOWN*

"A cup of wine, under the flowering trees;
I drink alone, for no friend is near.
Raising my cup I beckon the bright moon,
For he, with my shadow, will make three men.
The moon, alas, is no drinker of wine;
Listless, my shadow creeps about at my side.
Yet with the moon as friend and the shadow as slave
I must make merry before the Spring is spent.
To the songs I sing the moon flickers her beams;
In the dance I weave my shadow tangles and breaks.
While we were sober, three shared the fun;
Now we are drunk, each goes his way.
May we long share our odd, inanimate feast,
And meet at last on the Cloudy River of the sky."

—Li Po, Drinking Alone By Moonlight

FRANCESCO FERRARI
EXPLORES CHINATOWN

Li Po Cocktail Lounge
916 Grant Avenue
San Francisco, CA

Alleyways.

Alleyways are where the action is in San Francisco's Chinatown. The real action, that is. Always have been. Always will be—as I would soon discover. Dark and dank alleyways, sometimes squalid, sometimes sinister, sometimes dangerous, and largely narrow—just ten–to–15–feet wide, or less, in some places—so narrow that the sun scarcely sheds its light on them but for an hour or two at midday.

Chinatown herself, the city's most famous(or infamous)ethnic enclave, has been variously called the Chinese or *Oriental* quarter; the Chinese ghetto; the Celestial City; the *Oriental* City; the Flowery Kingdom; Little China; Little Canton; and even Canton of the West!

She's been variously perceived, too, as mysterious, secretive and sometimes sinister: a convoluted maze of flaring dragons, cluttered bazaars, cellar shops, foul–smelling fish and poultry markets, gambling and opium dens, tawdry brothels, disgusting dives, packed and dilapidated tenements with grated windows and grilled balconies illuminated by bright lanterns, all whispering in silent concert of romance and intrigue—a gaily painted sink and sewer of *Gum San Ta Fow*, that Big City in the Land of the Golden Mountains!

I'd been haunting the city's eminently *exotic, Oriental* quarter for some weeks, maybe months, drinking myself into senseless and shameless oblivion, ever since the young Catalonian woman I loved so deeply, Julieta, threw herself off the rooftop of the **San Francisco Armory** building—taking a cutthroat killer with her—to save my life.

I didn't really care much whether I lived or died. I figured that Chinatown might be the last place any of my caring and concerned friends—all three or four of them—would find me if they were really that caring and concerned enough even to look for me. And if you don't care for my *exotic–Oriental* terminology for characterizing the quaint little quarter, well, that's just tough! I was in no mood for anybody's politically correct bullshit, much less yours.

There was once a weekly newspaper—titled the *Tong Fan Goon Po*, or the **Oriental**—published for the Chinese in California by the missionary, William Speer, for which **Fung Afoo**, a Christianized Chinaman was the translator. That's just one minor example of why I abide by valid, historically factual, and *accurately* correct dictionary definitions—not any of your artificially contrived, supremely self–conscious, deeply in–denial, reality–avoidance, revisionist, phony–baloney, politically correct definitions. Got that? Good.

There's two drastically different and disparate Chinatowns, of course—the old and the new; the outmoded and modern. And the distinct line of demarcation differentiating them was that cataclysmic earthquake and fire of 1906—in which 28,000 structures were destroyed with an estimated death toll of 450. One of the more superficial of the numerous before–and–after earthquake changes—innovations, really—occurring in the quarter concerned Chinatown's lighting.

Old Chinatown was illuminated by those traditional red lanterns made of thin, translucent, varnished cheesecloth stretched tightly across bellied bamboo frames, splashed with black, green, and red Chinese characters—adages of goodwill that shone through brightly once soft tallow candles fired them to life to transform doorways and balconies into things of dimly–lit mysterious beauty.

New Chinatown innovated a wholly new medium with

fresh *exotic* values in the quarter: the *neon* light. It was left to the Chinese to group incredible color–blendings and designs with skillful creativity and astonishing originality. That *neon* light has imparted charm to the nocturnal aspects of the streets. With the passing of candle–lit lanterns, the restaurant balconies and other dim recesses grew garish with the white light of electric bulbs. But those *neon* lights gave the Chinese color to work with. The result is triumphant: cherry–blossom pinks, chrome yellows, ultramarine blues, apple greens, every shade and hue of orange and purple intermingle and blend together, flashing from the signs to entice tourists and visitors alike to the *exotic* enclave. All *exotic* merely means, incidentally, is *of foreign origin or character.* And anybody denying that distinctive attribute unique to this *Oriental* quarter is outright idiotic.

Dupont Street—the nucleus of old Chinatown which the Chinese called Dupont *Gai*—was known as the *Street of a Thousand Lanterns!* It was a scandalous street for a multitude of notorious reasons. So its notorious reaches have long since been renamed Grant Avenue for respectability's sake.

§

Just then, I was frequenting my newly favorite *neon*–irradiated dive bar for what felt like the thousandth time: the **Li Po**—so–called after its famous namesake, also known as ***Li Bai***, a celebrated Chinese poet of the Golden Age of Poetry in the Tang Dynasty; and by all accounts a serious drinker himself who celebrated in turn, amongst other enjoyments, the joys of drinking wine.

In mid–September, the ***Distribution of Moon Cakes*** festival is celebrated in honor of that inebriated poet, who reputedly went rowing on a lake one beautiful moonlit night after imbibing not wisely but all too well. Seeing the moon's reflection on the water, and thinking it a virtuously beautiful girl, he dove in after her and never came up. So every year as the season returns, the Chinese commemorate him by the simple rite of eating *rice cakes*—delicious dumplings made of rice flower, stuffed with chicken or pork and wrapped in green leaves.

§

Red for the Chinese is, of course, their lucky color. And the **Li Po** lounge abounds in red—from the tall radiant red **Li Po** lantern lettered in bright yellow, projecting overhead from the craggy front facade that looks something like the face of a rock–climbing wall, and overhanging the hefty double red–wooden doors opening out to the avenue from the golden–arched entryway; to the tall, red–topped stools lined up along the winding, polished bar stretching to the rearward corner shrine enclosing the grandiose, gleaming figure of a golden Chinese Buddha, illuminated by a pair of electric candelabrum, embraced by a pair of sturdy potted bamboo plants, a pair of lively and vigorous dragons, separated by a shiny bronze urn, on guard at his feet. That was my preferred, self–appointed drinking spot! It was close to closing and the bar comparatively quiet.

Personally, I was unkempt, unshaven, and downright slovenly. I looked like a bum, I felt like a bum, and to all intents and purposes, I bordered on being a bum. And I didn't give a damn. I was too high as a Chinese kite to care, I thought amusedly to myself.

Managing me at the moment was the bar manager—a handsome, trim, forty–something man with dark, closely shaven hair, a prodigious nose and ears, wearing a black sportshirt and a friendly smile—until, that is, I'd make him scowl with disapproval; which occurred pretty frequently throughout the night.

"Lookit, Fred," I rambled drunkenly, "you're sitting here—"

"You're sitting, Mister F.," he cut me short, correcting me stoically as he wiped up my latest spillage with spry swipes of his cloth, "We're *working!*"

"Don't quibble," I relented, heaving a heavy scoffing sigh. "Okay, then, you're *standing* here in the center of the notorious Barbary Coast! It's a compact area bounded by Montgomery Street on the east, Stockton Street on the west, Broadway on the north, and Washington Street on the south where the cheap brothels and cribs were commonly found. Pacific Street was the heart of the Barbary Coast! That's only a couple blocks from here! Dupont Street was still the Chinese district. It was the haunt of the vicious and vile of every sort! Every conceivable kind of crime, vice, and villainy went down there! It was nine square blocks of sheer murder and mayhem!"

"There's about to be two square feet of murder and mayhem right here in a minute," the Chinese barman I called Fred jeered.

"Very funny," I remarked with a shitfaced grin, "you're a riot, Fred, a real riot."

Three youthful twenty–something Chinese barmaids labored along with Fred tending bar: two were petite, sweet–faced, smiling babes I called Jacqueline and Winifred. The third was known only as the *Mai–Tai Queen*— a racy–looking, petite but shapely young gal sporting a low–cut, form–fitting black sweater. Her breast–length, uncommonly brown hair fringed her soft, perfectly oval face. For a Chinese chick, she had an almost aquiline nose, plus this endearing habit of squinting her eyes beneath her thinly arched brows—yes, even more squinty than normal—and tightly pursing her thin lips to express her displeasure at something, like me as a rule.

"He's dredging up ancient history again," the Queen cracked as she stepped up to my place at the bar.

"I'm a student of history!" I exclaimed. "The real Barbary Coast was an African pirate's lair! It's fascinating stuff!"

"You, my dear," I whispered conspiratorially, leaning closely across the bartop, "could've been an inmate of a house of ill fame! San Francisco was once a very sinful and wicked place!"

"Now he's calling me a prostitute," she said, conspicuously perturbed.

"No!" I promptly contradicted her. "Not you! Your great, great, great, great, great grandmother, maybe, but not you!"

"Do you want another Mai–Tai?" she asked me with a shake of her head, ignoring my remark.

"Of course I want another Mai–Tai!" I blurted out brashly. "That's what I'm here for! Thank you, sweetheart!"

"Don't call me sweetheart!" she huffed, snapping up my empty goblet.

"Oh!" I groaned beneath my breath with a dismissive wave of my hand. "What do you want me to call you— *Dragon Lady*?"

After all, that trademark Chinese Mai–Tai was to the **Li Po** what Irish coffee was to the *Buena Vista Cafe*, my old beloved homestead, which I hadn't seen for many a long day.

"Anyway," I said, turning back to Fred to continue spouting my drunken discourse, "there was this extreme disparity between the sexes in those times! There were thousands of Chinese men but only a few Chinese women—and most of those were prostitutes! The male–to–female ratio was almost 30–to–one at one point!"

"That's very interesting, Professor F.," Fred remarked

with a slightly sarcastic smile.

"They didn't call it the *bachelor society* for nothing!" I ran on as the Queen returned to deliver my umpteenth Mai–Tai and snatch the cash I plunked down onto the bartop. "Thank you, honey!"

"Don't call me honey!"

"She not only makes the meanest Mai–Tai on the planet," I driveled, "she's super *sexy* to boot—as in *booty*!"

"Don't harass the staff," Fred admonished me calmly.

"I'm not harassing her!" I protested. "I'm *complimenting* her! Why can't people take compliments graciously anymore?"

"Maybe she wants to be appreciated for something other than her looks," the super pretty barmaid, Jacqueline, paused to stoop to say softly.

"Oh!" I drawled in a derisive tone of voice, maundering madly. "Have I offended your little sensibilities? And the whole wide world is supposed to care about what she wants, right? So, what? She wants to be admired for her *mind*? Well, let me fill you in on just a few basic facts of life: the world doesn't give a tinker's damn about what she or anybody else wants! And expecting it to ever conform to what you want is both impractical and unrealistic. Accept the world for what it is—just *crap*—otherwise you're bound to be deeply disappointed!"

"Besides," I harped on, still scurrilous as hell, "her *mind* is hardly the most transparent thing about her to spectators across this bar now is it? Her exterior attributes are obviously the more conspicuous! So if somebody happens to compliment them, it wouldn't kill you to be gracious enough to just accept the compliment and move on with your little life! There's plenty more important things in life to fret about!"

"Are you all right, Mister F.?" Fred the bartender asked me abruptly, reaching out to gently place his warm palm on my shoulder—sensing, I'm sure, that I was indeed a man in mournful pain. The Chinese are nothing if not exceptionally perceptive and empathetic.

"No," I bowed my head, shaking it, emphatic, with a low groan. "I'm not all right."

"Maybe you should go home now, Mister F.?" he suggested just as gently.

"If I had a home to go to," I snickered, satirically. "I have no home, Mister Fred."

Suddenly, out of the corner of my drunken eye, I caught a glimpse of a pair of young dour and tough–looking Chinese men—sporting, strangely, traditional throwback merchant–class black *changshan* tunics! Had they possessed long braided queues—pigtails to the unacquainted—their retro look would've been picture–perfect; but their hair was as dark as their tunics and close–cropped. They sat together on low–set metal chairs at a round table in the bar's dimly lit rearward section nearby, their hands clasped on the tabletop. Their features wore intensely stern expressions. And I was getting the distinct impression that they were staring—scowling severely—straight at me!

"Get a load of those two!" I told Fred in a low, mocking voice, nodding my head in their direction. "Now there's a couple of sketchy characters! Maybe they're a couple of hoodlums!"

"Not so loud, Mister F.!" Fred said, glancing around nervously and wiping the bartop choppily.

"Don't look at me, Fred," I told him with my most facetious tone, poking at the bartop for emphasis, "leave it to the *Irish* to invent the concept and practice of hooliganism. It shouldn't come as any surprise whatsoever that the term *hoodlum* was coined right here in this town!"

Just then though, quite unexpectedly, something plenty more pleasant and pleasing caught my drunkenly roving eye: I caught sight of the most comely young Chinese girl sitting at the bar a couple of stools away from me, caressing a full glass of a *Li Po Special,* a bent straw jutting from its frothy top. Since she was facing away from me, her elbow resting on the bartop, the fingertips of her other hand bracing her chin, I could only pore over her captivating profile—but I could still tell, instinctively, that she was strikingly beautiful!

Just as the Arabs imagine their feminine ideal, alluding to such aspects as doe–shaped eyes and pomegranate–shaped breasts, so do the Chinese conceive of their own ideal of Chinese beauty: composed of graceful, almond–shaped eyes; brows like crescent–shaped moons; lips gracefully curved like the banana; a face flushed like the peach leaf; her wrists round and as white as her ivory bracelet; her fingers delicate and tapering—this young gal I was ogling had it all, trust me!

This Chinese girl I was gazing at was completely covered—she wore a neck–high black top underneath a gray alpaca sweater and was striking a pensive pose and looking opposite. Her gleaming black hair was pulled back into a tight bun positioned perfectly at the nape of her neck. Tasselated earrings dangled from her long lobes. Her cheek and neck looked exceptionally soft and smooth, pale but bursting with youthful bloom.

"All right, Fred," I finally relented, swiping the bartop awkwardly. "I'll call it a night. But before I go, I'll see if there's somebody else in this place who can take a compliment graciously—"

Unsteadily, I got to my feet to leave.

"Goodnight, Mister F.," Fred bid me. "Take care of yourself."

Nodding, I raised a limp–wristed hand to wave weakly as I beat my drunken retreat.

"Excuse me, miss," I started, coming up quietly behind that comely young Chinese girl, sitting so contemplatively at the bar.

Taken by surprise, and looking slightly startled, she took the unspoken but full, miserable measure of me.

"Forgive me for intruding on your reflections," I told her as contritely as I could, stammering slightly, "but I just felt compelled to compliment you—on the incredibly sublime beauty of your...*profile*."

"Thank you," she said reluctantly, after looking askance at me, speechless, for some moments.

"That's all right," I said, holding up my hands, apologetic. "You're welcome. Goodnight."

Then I directed my eyes to Fred the bartender, who stood aghast watching the entire encounter, and I nodded knowingly at him, another shitfaced grin on my face.

"See," I muttered to myself as I turned on my heel, stumbling toward the exit to head out. "See."

§

Unbeknownst to me at the time, those two young Chinese toughs sitting in the rear of the **Li Po** bar had got up to follow me outside. Then came that famous, fuming San Francisco fog as moving veils of sea mist started to obscure the murky streets and alleys of the *Oriental* quarter. Shakily hugging the grilled storefronts, I'd crossed the street and was shuffling on southward along Grant, an avenue so narrow, and packed with perpetually parked cars that never seemed to move, that it was a one–way byway for vehicular traffic; in those parking spaces was where Chinese street vendors had once set up their awning–covered stalls for selling sacks of rice and crates of perishable produce—like baskets of foot–long green beans.

This was the modern, new Chinatown, where laundry still drooped from metal fire escapes and never–forgotten pungent scents of sizzling wok oil, dried fish, and sausages still drifted throughout the quarter once known as Little Canton. As did perfume from hand–carved camphor chests and *exotic* China–imported teas, mingling with the tantalizing smells of moon cakes and warm custard tarts. Those quaint cobblestoned streets of times past were long since paved over with asphalt. Shopkeepers replaced the red curtains and wooden planks they once pulled across their entrances with pane glass windows and barred doors.

By the 1930s—if you're still in deep denial about the quarter's distinctive *Oriental* nature—Grant Avenue, once those glaring *neon* signs replaced those delicate paper lanterns, had transformed itself into a glamorous night-spot. Chinese bars and cocktail lounges materialized, trailed by equally *exotic* nightclubs like **Forbidden City**, the **Kubla Khan**, and **Shangri–La**. Getting educated can eradicate all denial.

If you think those fighting tongs are things of the remote past then think again—though admittedly their fighting element is less prevalent nowadays.

Just across the street from the **Li Po** bar at 925 Grant Avenue stands the lone grey metal–plated glass door opening up to the stairway leading to the *Suey Sing Tong*, also known as the *Hall of Auspicious Victory*, whose original namesake has a quaint little history all its own: founded by *Yee Low Dai*, and kept united by leaders like the scholarly poet, *Hong Ah Kay*, who was credited by tongman, *Eng Ying(Eddie)Gong*, with being the high-binder who changed the modus operandi of the notorious hatchet men from ax or cleaver to the revolver!

These were discomforting thoughts to be turning over in my drunken mind as I was threading my way slowly past those tall, ornamental, ultramarine lamp posts set at evenly spaced intervals along the avenue, lined with so many darkened gift, import, jewelry, and souvenir shops.

As I was approaching Washington, the oncoming cross street—it was then that I finally sensed the presence of those two toughs, who were following me at a discreet distance. I'd long been slipping as a private detective, but drunk or sober I could still spot such an over–obvious tail as those two! Staggering, I rounded the right corner at Washington Street, another narrow one–way byway— passing by the **Buddha Lounge**, another recent haunt of mine—and bent my shaky steps westward. **Magical Ice Cream** shop, at the facing corner at 900 Grant Avenue, was once the **Wing Lee Company**, a hardware store owned by *Wong See Duck*, a member of that powerful *Suey Sing Tong*; the store was a front for importing Chinese sex–slave girls. More restaurants and trading companies inhabited this street.

I deliberately bypassed old infamous Pike Street, now known as *Waverly Place*, or *Ho Boon Gai* or *Fifteen Cent Street*, across the street to the left, out of superstitious solicitude if nothing else. Fifteen cents was once the cost of haircuts at the many barber shops lining those streets.

At the **San Sun** Restaurant, at the closest corner to the right, I ducked into Ross Alley, or old Stout's Alley, once nicknamed the *Street of the Gamblers*, where *Chin Tin Sen*, alias *Tom Chu*, called the *King of Gamblers*, once lived. Beneath their flickering electric lights at nightfall, Chinatown's alleyways turn ghost–like from the ocean's breath blown from the dunes in a pallid cloud.

On either side, this profoundly narrow alleyway was lined with weatherbeaten buildings of faded red and ocher–colored brick three and five stories high. Barred doors and windows hollowed the walls. Metal balconies and fire escapes hung overhead. Tall, slender, black lamp posts threw but dim and shadowed light upon the alleyway. I ducked into the cramped, brick–lined niche of the first barred doorway that I came to. Dirty tiles scuffed underfoot. I stood shiveringly still—breathless, petrified, my temples throbbing—waiting with bated breath.

Then, of all people, I got to thinking about **Fung Jing Toy**, sometimes called *Fong Chong*, and otherwise known as **Little Pete**, the notorious criminal *Gi Sin Seer Tong* or *Guild of Hereditary Virtue* leader and onetime *King of Chinatown*! His third–floor home had been located directly opposite at 819–1/2 Washington Street! Worse than that, the very barber shop where he was ignominiously assassinated by a pair of tong gunmen had been located just two doors down at 817 Washington Street! So when he was mercilessly murdered, he sat near the door in a barber's chair facing—and probably watching—Ross Alley! Now the frightening, present-day irony was: I was practically staring, wide–eyed, at that terrible spot where Little Pete got himself killed!

I waited for a fairly long while before finally emerging from that doorway after hearing no footfalls following after me. No sooner had I stepped into the alleyway, naturally, did those two robustly–built toughs step sedately—and forebodingly—into view from either side of the alleyway outlet. In hand, more ominously, they each grasped the sawed–off, hole–cut handle of a *hatchet* some six inches long—glinting menacingly in the faint lamplight.

"Oh, shit!" I muttered despairingly to myself.

"Good evening, gentlemen," I greeted them drunkenly but as mirthfully as I could muster, smiling feebly, "are you sure we can't *calmly* talk this over—whatever's distressing you?"

Far from acting placated, they started moving toward me, looking equally laconic and determined in demeanor.

From beneath my rumpled jacket, I awkwardly drew from its shoulder holster my *Smith & Wesson*, stainless steel, seven–shot, 686P model, .357 revolver with the four–inch barrel, aiming at them unsteadily.

"Lookit," I warned them sternly, "I don't want to use this so don't make me shoot! Just beat it!"

Without warning, the one tough forcefully flung his hatchet straight at me—accurately striking my gun and knocking it from my hand—both weapons clattering to the cement! His right arm and hatchet upraised, the other tough charged and flung *himself* at me—his left hand clutching at my throat! To strike that hatchet into my head, he chopped downward with his right arm, which I weakly caught with a karate X–block, driving my crossed hands upwards as tight fists. With a frequently practiced reaction, I immediately grabbed his chopping arm, wrenching him forward and downward, twisting my torso forcefully to the right as I delivered a drunken front knee kick, driving my rearward right leg hard into his groin, twisting my torso to the left once more. Groaning aloud, but hardly fazed, the attacking tough struck at me with a forceful *back*swing of the hatchet—deeply slashing my right chest! I cried out in searing pain, agonized and outraged. And as he swung past me, his faced exposed, I forcefully drove a hard right palm–heel strike straight into his bloodied nose—losing my balance and stumbling to the ground in the process!

Splayed out on my back, propped up by my elbows, I shook my head deliriously and slowly but surely lifted up my bleary eyes to see the most startling sight: the other tough hovering squarely over me and leveling my own revolver directly at me! Watching my own gun pointed at me, staring down its black barrel, its bullet–loaded chamber starting to roll—I lost all leftover hope, all leftover heart, and felt all the despair of the world cave in on me like a massive millstone!

My name's Francesco Ferrari. I'm a private detective. Or at least I was—once. And this was when I was down and out in Chinatown!

ONE: SAVED BY AN ANGEL

"One who excels as a warrior does not appear formidable;
One who excels in fighting is never aroused by anger;
One who excels in defeating his enemy does not join issue;
One who excels in employing others humbles himself before them;
This is known as the virtue of non-contention;
This is known as making use of the efforts of others;
This is known as matching the sublimity of heaven."
—Lao Tzu, Tao Te Ching, Book Two, LXVIII

FRANCESCO FERRARI
EXPLORES CHINATOWN

Shouts heard in the streets of Chinatown were sometimes referred to as *echoes*! But what saved my life that night was the outcry of a celestial angel!

"No!" came the shrill shriek from the feminine voice, echoing throughout the alleyway's confines. "Don't!"

And the Chinese tough wielding my gun tugged frantically at the tunic of his cohort, who was pawing his bloodied nose, and they both absconded together from the mouth of that alleyway posthaste.

Wincing in pain, I lifted up my eyes in a tight squint, straining to make out who screamed in just the nick of time. I picked out the tall, well–formed but stiffened, feminine figure silhouetted against the lurid, shadowed light shed from the other end of the alleyway. Slowly but surely, she stepped up into the somber spot of dim lamplight thrown upon the asphalt, hesitating to betray herself. And at first glance, all I could see of her was the graceful, pale curve of her long leg laid bare by the high–necked, shape–squeezing, thigh–split, satiny red, embroidered silk *cheongsam* she was wearing.

"Are you all right?" she asked me, caringly, letting fall the two pale and delicate hands she had thrown up to her mouth in mortal fear at the frightful sight she'd just witnessed.

"That's the second time somebody's asked me that tonight," I answered with a tortured chuckle, shaking my head and clutching my chest, blood seeping through my fingers, "but no, I'm most definitely not all right."

"I'll call for help!" she volunteered, promptly producing that ubiquitous mobile telephone.

"No!" I cried out, throwing up my bloodied hand in anguished protest. "No police! I'll call a cabbie buddy of mine. You've stuck your neck out enough for one night!"

"A cab?" she remarked, incredulous, drawing nearer,

warily. "But you're hurt! You're bleeding! You need help!"

"I'll be okay," I muttered doubtfully. "It's not that bad—I don't think."

"I don't think you're thinking straight! You need to make sure! You could bleed to death!"

"Well," I chuckled halfheartedly, groaning aloud, "thanks, but, that just might be for the best. Just make yourself scarce. Don't get yourself into trouble. I'll take care of myself."

"That's crazy talk! At least let me help you stop up that wound!"

"What are you—a quack or something? Lookit, honestly, I just don't care anymore."

"Well, I do!" she persisted. "And I'm not about to just let you lie there and bleed to death! You're coming with me!"

"Coming?" I chuckled again, groaning drunkenly. "Coming where?"

"With me," she repeated. "I live here in the alley."

And with that, she bowed down and reached out to me her outstretched hands and arms, grasping me tightly by my armpits, struggling to help me stand up.

§

She wasn't exaggerating, either. She literally lived in Ross Alley—in a self–contained in–law apartment otherwise known as a secondary suite or accessory dwelling unit—hers situated at grade about midway in that alleyway. And once she got me to my feet, draping my left arm around her shoulder, she led me, grunting and staggering, to the narrow metal door sidled by the slender faded brass mailbox indenting the alley wall.

In–law flats in San Francisco are generally lengthy structures, stretching endwise through their main buildings with rooms and living spaces constructed crosswise along the span of the elongated dwellings. Just inside her front door, which she hastily locked behind us, we stepped inside a small foyer enclosing her flat's laundry with twin washing machines. Setting foot on the narrow, musty, dimly–lit, and drab carpeted hallway, she guided me along to the flat's leftward little bathroom, situated just opposite its little kitchen and pantry.

"Sit there," she directed me, gesturing to the nearby toilet seat, which I plunked myself down on. Unabashedly, she helped me wriggle out of my jacket and blood–soaked shirt, throwing them aside. She hurriedly rummaged through her medicine cabinet, plucking out a gauze bandage to plaster against the gaping gash in my chest, seeping pretty profusely with blood, which opened widely like some evenly incised–and–severed eye!

"Hold that and apply pressure to the wound!" she directed me as I splayed myself out indifferently against the back of that toilet seat.

"Yes, ma'am," I scoffed, feebly holding the bandage to the bleeding wound. "Are you one of those big–footed women?"

"Don't waste my time, dammit!" she scolded me. "Press it hard!"

I obliged, straining to sit up more erect and attentive.

"That's better!" she said, plucking out a plastic brown bottle and a plastic–capped tube—directly drenching the wound with the antiseptic hydrogen peroxide solution and smearing it liberally with the antibiotic cream before finally applying a fresh dressing; sealing it snugly with *First Aid* tape.

"Gawd, that hurts!" I griped.

"It should!"

"Where did you learn to do all that?"

"When you work with Chinese cooks and waiters who

quarrel with meat cleavers," she said with a giggle, "you pick up special skills."

"Then you're not one of those slanty–eyed Orientals right off the boat?"

"No, I'm not," she said, perturbed, washing and wringing her hands. "So don't press your luck, mister. You've only been here five minutes and you're already wearing out your welcome."

"I'm sorry. I'm not always this obnoxious."

"Happy to hear it."

"Sometimes I really work at it."

"I bet you do. Come and lie down and rest for now," she invited me. "I'll make you some tea."

Once more, she helped me struggle to get up and stagger along as she led me to the darkened bedroom at the rearmost part of the in–law apartment, guiding me with care to a sturdy full–over–full futon bunk bed.

"You have a roommate then?" I asked her.

"No, just a close friend who comes to stay with me sometimes."

"Oh," I groaned as she helped me recline on the bottom bunk futon, patting down the pillow for me and spreading a quilted coverlet over me.

Finally, I could fully contemplate the ideal Chinese beauty Rachel's faultless face, embraced by her straight, shoulder–length, blueblack hair, was possessed of: the all-graceful almond eyes, crescent brows, dainty nose, pleasing lips, and peachy complexion—her most captivating and becoming quality being her ever–present *pensive* expression!

"Never mind the tea for the moment if you don't mind," I bid her, taking one of her resisting hands warmly in both of mine. "Tell me why you're doing all this."

"I've always had a soft spot for helping strays in trouble," she joked, shrinking slightly as she withdrew her hand and sat down in a wicker chair close by the bunk. "Why do you drink so much?"

"I'd rather not talk about that," I said, dismissive. "Let's just say that it has something to do with wanting to die but not having the guts to off myself."

"That sounds serious," she said, looking worried. "So what's your name?"

"Ferrari. Francesco Ferrari. But you can call me Frank."

"Oh, no. I prefer Francesco."

"So did my grandmother—on my father's side. She emigrated to Boston from Naples. Your choice is fine."

"Italiano, huh? Well, Mister Francesco, you should take better care of yourself. You would be a pretty handsome man if you spruced yourself up a little."

"And you, my dear, look like a lovely China Doll."

"Oh, no. Don't call me that."

"Now what's wrong with that? A true China Doll is an antique of rare and incomparable beauty."

"I think *you're* an antique, Mister Francesco."

"You might be right about that," I chuckled good–naturedly. "So what's your name?"

"Rachel."

"That's pretty—like you. Rachel what?"

"Rachel Chung."

"What's your given name, I mean."

"How do you know Rachel's not my given name?"

"Well, I don't. But in my experience in this city, a lot of immigrants in this area adopt Americanized names."

"So naturally you assume that I'm an immigrant?"

"Don't get touchy about it. It's just a curious question. Fact is, we're *all* immigrants in some form or other; you're hardly special in that regard. Even the so–called *Native* Americans are immigrants. They probably crossed the Bering Strait from southern Siberia to come here for

Crissakes!"

"You've got a point there, Mister Francesco—but just the one. But, yes, I'm an immigrant of sorts. I'm here on a student visa from Taiwan."

"Ah, Formosa—the beautiful island, as it was known in Portuguese."

"An educated man."

"Not really—more like a mind that's a repository for a ton of unimportant trivia."

"I'm sure you know many things of importance."

"You flatter me, but thank you, I do appreciate it."

"And I appreciate your appreciation of me."

"You're Taiwanese then?"

"No!" she exclaimed, adamant. "I'm a *Chinese* who happens to come from Taiwan."

"I'm sorry, I didn't mean to offend. So, do you adopt an Americanized name out of conformity or convenience?"

"A little of both, perhaps. But truth be told, it's mostly because Americans cannot properly pronounce Chinese names."

"So, you think we're pretty stupid, huh?"

"Not stupid—just linquistically challenged!"

"Your Chinese name being?" I asked, finally feeling reason enough to laugh aloud.

"Shih–Tseng."

"I have a good musical ear, let me try it: Shih–Tseng."

"*Shih*–Tseng," she repeated with emphasis.

"*Shih*–Tseng," I repeated, mimicking her.

"Not bad. My first adopted name was Alice."

"Alice?"

"Yes. Who knows? I may adopt another American name if I become fond of a different one."

"That could prove to be pretty confusing to some people. I knew it all along though."

"Knew what?"

"That you're one of those *singing* girls?"

"Sing–*Song* girls, you mean. I've heard of them."

"Exactly. I read a fascinating book recently titled *Alice*. It was all about the memoirs of a Barbary Coast prostitute who was Chinese!"

"So sorry to disappoint: but I'm just a restaurant hostess who goes to school on the side."

"You're beautiful enough though to have been a *Daughter of Joy*," I heartened her.

"A what?"

"Another name the singing girls used to be called: a Daughter of Joy. Are you joy*ful*?"

"No, I'm not," again adamant. "So don't get any ideas in that area while you're here, Mister Francesco."

"Oh, no, I won't—I mean, I wouldn't," I reassured her. "Besides, I'm much too incapacitated to get any ideas in that direction."

"That's good—just as long as things stay that way."

"They will, I promise. But you know what?"

"What, Mister Francesco?"

"There's something else the singing girls used to be called."

"What's that, Mister Francesco?"

"Fair but frail. And that's what you are, dearest Alice—*fair but frail...*"

I strained every nerve trying to reach out and gently touch—caress, really—Rachel's flushed cheek.

One of the most unhappiest, joy*less*, and profoundly sad things in all the world is watching a tear falling out of an *Oriental* eye. An all–consuming delirium and fatigue finally combined to completely and utterly numb every last nerve in my body. So as I blacked out, sinking into mindless oblivion, I never saw the gentle, untrammeled tear that welled out of Rachel's *Oriental* eye—and flowed ever so softly down the full side of her joyless face.

TWO:
AWAKE IN THE ASPHALT JUNGLE

"Have in your hold the great image
And the empire will come to you.
Coming to you and meeting with no harm
It will be safe and sound.
Music and food
Will induce the wayfarer to stop.
The way in its passage through the mouth is
without flavour.
It cannot be seen.
It cannot be heard.
Yet it cannot be exhausted by use."
—Lao Tzu, Tao Te Ching, Book One, XXXV

FRANCESCO FERRARI
EXPLORES CHINATOWN

Lions and Tigers and Bears, Oh My!

I awoke in Rachel's in–law bunk bed with quite a start, sensing myself—strangely—surrounded by lions and tigers and bears right out of that American musical fantasy film from Metro Goldwyn–Mayer of 1939: the *Wizard of Oz*! Just as Dorothy, the Scarecrow, and the Tin Man were meeting the cowardly Lion! Well, maybe not so many bears as such, on second thought. No tigers, either, I must admit.

What I did actually wake up to once I did finally manage to sit up, severely sluggish and bleary–eyed, was the profoundly diversified fauna and flora of *Africa*, the world's second–largest and second–most populated continent! All around me, on all sides, stood out in dramatic relief, a vast variety of lions, leopards, rhinos, hippos, cheetahs, giraffes, elephants—and, of course, zebras—plus a sizable assortment of African grasslands, deserts, forests, highlands, savannas, and woodlands! Inexplicably, I was wholly immersed in...*Africa*!

It's a *jungle* in here, I muttered to myself!

What I was really seeing, of course, were numerous African representations or depictions, blown–up picture–prints hung all over the room and only dimly illuminated by the faint light shed by a couple of matted windows!

Next to the bunk bed, atop the nightstand, I promptly noticed the conspicuously placed piece of writing paper disclosing the neatly penned note, which I snapped up to read:

> *Francesco,*
> *Refresh yourself.*
> *I will return shortly.*
> *Rachel*

Stranger still, next to the note I found a stainless steel, pan–and–body, double–halved military *mess kit*! I unfolded its handle from the metal kit's central divider and un-latched its secure center lid ring to lay open its meat can body—containing, I discovered, its meat ration: a goodly portion of delectably fresh Chinese *mincemeat*, which I started eating with gusto with the stray spoon left atop the table. I'm in the Army now, I thought amusedly to myself, washing down the food with the Chinese herbal tea left in the dainty, porcelain twin–set cup and teapot. This was either one exceptionally eccentric or one excep-tionally unique young girl I was suddenly ensconced with!

Piled atop the table, too, were a triple set of paperback books I picked up to shuffle through and peruse their cov-ers: perhaps unsurprisingly, a copy of *Out of Africa*, that famous 1937 memoir by Danish writer, Karen Blixen, oth-erwise known as Isak Dinesen, her pen name; a copy of the *Tao Te Ching* by the Old Master Chinese Taoist philoso-pher, Lao Tzu; and strangest of all, a bright tiny red copy of that famous(or infamous)Little Red Book, the collected speeches, statements, and writings of Mao Tse–tung, also known as Mao Zedong, the former Chairman of the Chi-nese Communist Party titled, *Quotations From Chairman Mao TseTung*, first published around 1966 and widely dis-tributed during China's so–called Cultural Revolution!

Behind the books was propped a wooden–glass pic-ture–frame displaying, surprisingly, a tablet proclama-tion of principles by **Sun Yat–sen**, the famous Chinese statesman and political philosopher who served as the first leader of the Kuomintang, or Nationalist Party of China, and the provisional first president of the Republic of Chi-na, where he's called the Father of the Nation:

"For forty years I have devoted myself to the cause of the people's revolution with but one aim in view— the elevation of China to a position of freedom and equality among the nations. My experiences during these forty years have fully convinced me that to at-

tain this goal we must bring about a thorough awak-
ening of our own people and ally ourselves in a com-
mon struggle with those peoples of the world who
treat us on an equal basis so that they may cooperate
with us in our struggles.
The work of the Revolution is not yet over. All my
comrades must continue to exert their efforts ac-
cording to my Programme of National Reconstruc-
tion, Outline of Reconstruction, the Three Principles
of the People, and the Manifesto issued by the First
National Congress of our Party, and strive on ear-
nestly for the consummation of the end we have in
view. Above all, our recent declarations in favour of
the convocation of a People's Convention and the ab-
olition of unequal treaties should be carried into ef-
fect with the least possible delay. This is my heartfelt
charge to you."
(Signed)Sun Wen
February 20, 1925

Late, I noticed my once slashed–and–bloodied shirt
washed, dried, neatly folded and placed alongside me atop
the futon mattress. How incredibly kind, I thought. I put
on the shirt, buttoning it up—fingering the searingly sore
but bandaged gash in my chest through the shirt's slashed
cloth.

This was one very unique young girl, indeed. My curiosity sufficiently aroused, I got up to perform a cursory
inspection of the rest of her room to discover just how
unique: and in another recess of the room stood an elegant
Guzheng, or Chinese plucked zither, a large, resonant 64–
inch soundboard with some 26 strings composed of Pau-
lownia wood—a Chinese musical stringed instrument of
exceptionally pleasing timbre. Surrounding that zither
stood a cluster of art easels supporting canvas paintings,
depicting skillful realistic renditions of brilliantly colorful

flowers and water lilies.

In another corner of the room, finally, I came across an enlarged poster–print of **Chung Kuei**, or **Zhong Kui**, a Chinese deity who's traditionally regarded as a vanquisher of ghosts and evil beings! That was when Rachel returned to pleasantly surprise me.

"*Chung Kuei* could reputedly command eighty thousand demons!" she enlightened me. "He's a very righteous guardian! Chinese families often paint his image on the doors of their houses as a guardian spirit, or even at places of business where costly goods are traded. He protects them from evil demons and scares off ghosts, too."

"He sounds like quite a formidable fellow," I remarked. "He must've been in attendance at last night's festivities, I imagine—thankfully, I should say."

Rachel bowed her head, her hands clasped behind her back, smiling shyly. She was wearing more traditional dress, her *cheongsam* gone. Then she lifted up those penetrating but pensive almond eyes of hers to meet mine in an awkward moment of still quiet.

"So, how do you feel today?" she asked me.

"Oh," I answered, adamant yet abashed, gesturing around the room "much, much better thanks to you! You saved my life in more ways than one—both figuratively and literally, I should say! So I thank you—profusely— for everything! The safe refuge, the medical attention, the food, the clean shirt—everything! That mincemeat was delicious, by the way, and that mess kit made me feel like a right proper G.I. Joe even though I've never been a soldier! I'm deep in your debt! I'm very sorry that I was in such a state that I didn't even thank you last night. I hope you'll pardon me for that. And I apologize—sincerely."

Again, she bowed her head, shaking it slightly, saying nothing.

"Well," I started, reluctantly, "I shouldn't impose on

you any further. I guess I should go before I start blub-
bering—"

Hastily, I plucked out my calling card from my pocket
and plunked it down onto that nightstand. Then I stepped
straight up to her and waited, expectantly, for her to lift
up her eyes to me once more.

"That's my card," I stammered, gesturing nervously to the tabletop. "If there's anything I can ever do for
you—anything at all—I hope you won't hesitate to—I
mean, I hope you'll please call me."

"Two things," she said simply, and softly, once she did
look up again.

"Two things?"

"Yes—two things you can do for me."

"What things—anything."

"First," she told me quite deliberately, "you can take a
lot better care of yourself in the future."

"And second?"

"Second," she told me with the slightest hint of innocent flirtation, "you can stay and talk with me for a little
while—after you clean yourself up, of course."

§

"You're a girl after my own heart, Rachel!" I told her
after she'd set up a pair of folding chairs at a worktable for
us to share together a couple of rice bowls, simmering with
some piping-hot Chinese noodles she'd prepared for us to
eat. Her Chinese bowls were like her—extremely delicate:
glazed deep apple-green with pink blossoms traced on the
outer surfaces with yellow birds twittering from cherry
branches.

Before she sat down across from me, she'd switched
on a shelved compact disc player, playing the musical
soundtrack to the American epic romantic drama film

from 1985 composed by famous English film composer, John Barry: *Out of Africa*!

"Oh, really?" she asked me coyly. "Why's that?"

"John Barry's my all–time favorite composer—ever!" I exclaimed excitedly. "He deservedly won the Academy Award Oscar for Best Original Score for his *Out of Africa* soundtrack, I know! I love his score to the film, *Somewhere In Time*, even more; so incredibly emotional. His music is so surreal. It has such an unearthly quality to it."

"I agree," she said, gesturing about between mouthfuls, which we were plucking up with our pairs of wooden chopsticks. "It always helps me set the mood and atmosphere for *my* Africa!"

"*Your* Africa?"

"Someplace I've always craved to travel to but could never afford—so I travel there vicariously through *my* Africa, right here!"

"Yes," I joked, glancing around, "I did notice the preoccupation with the place! It's a vast continent. Any particular part of it of special interest to you?"

"*All* of it!" she said.

"Then you'll make it there someday," I encouraged her, pausing to look at her thoughtfully.

"You're a girl of many extraordinary talents, too—what with all the art and the zither and whatnot!" I went on to compliment her. "You painted all those pretty pictures, I take it?"

"Yes," she nodded. "the water lillies are painted from the *Lily Pond* at *Golden Gate Park*. It's my absolute favorite spot in all of San Francisco. I visit there often."

"I adore the park, too," I started timidly. "Perhaps we could take a picnic there sometime."

"Yes," she looked up, smiling warmly, "that might be nice."

"There's one thing I'm very curious about, though,

that I have to ask you," I told her, abruptly changing the subject.

"Oh," she asked, slightly apprehensive, "what's that?"

"Those books on your nightstand," I mentioned, thumbing toward her bunk bed. "Now the Africa book I can understand. What I don't get, though, is a framed proclamation by Sun Yat–sen set up next to Mao Tse–tung's *Little Red Book!*"

"What's wrong with that?"

"Nothing's wrong with it. It's just slightly...politically...*incongruous!*"

"Oh, that!" she cackled aloud. "Well, I'm still a believer in the nationalist revolution. Sun Yat–sen's story is especially sad. He devoted his life to a better, more peaceful and prosperous China but died of a broken heart. The *Little Red Book* is just a constant little reminder...to *know thine enemy!*"

"The last time I looked," I told her, "the *Kuomintang* National Chinese Party still has its headquarters in the city over on Stockton Street."

"Yes, I know."

"Do you intend to stay here—in the states, I mean," I asked her, changing the subject.

"We displaced exiles from mainland China consider ourselves to be the *wandering* Chinese even though we have our island homeland of Taiwan," she said, sadly. "To ever reunite all our peoples still seems like a dream as remote as the moon. But I'll return home eventually after I finish my studies here. I hadn't planned on anything but a temporary stay here if that's what you mean; I wasn't planning on settling here or making a permanent home here—no."

"Ah, you're one of those *sojourners* then."

"What's that?"

"In a nutshell—a transient migrant who comes to

America to clean up and exploit the country for its various benefits before returning to their fatherland. Here today and gone tomorrow!"

"That's a little simplistic, my dear Francesco," Rachel chuckled. "If you only knew the exorbitant fees the *Academy of Art College* charges its international students then you'd know that *I'm* the one being exploited!"

"That's different," I kidded her knowingly. "Those overpriced foreign fees are necessary, you see, to subsidize all those sprawling real estate investments all over the city so essential to expanding the Academy's provincial empire!"

"A most astute analysis, Mister Francesco."

"Then you don't aspire to become one of those chronically complaining Asian–Americans constantly whining about the supposed trials and tribulations of assimilation!"

"No, I most definitely do not!" she answered, most adamant. "I'd much rather remain a proud *gum san hock* than ever become a *juk sing* living in the land of the *fan kwei*!"

"Now you've really lost me!"

"Ah!" Rachel heaved a heavy sigh. "Like I said—linguistically challenged! A *gum san hock* is a returnee to China from the *gum shan*—the mountain of gold. A *juk sing* is a scorned American–born Chinese neighbor. And *fan kwei*, of course, are the American foreign devils. So I'll leave you to fill in the blanks!"

"Of course!" I cried, laughing aloud, clapping my hands with laughter–loving glee—something I hadn't felt or experienced in many moons! "Well, on that note!—"

Just then, there came another, different and more intrusive—even ominous—sound; noise, really: a rackety, obnoxious, and persistent banging at the front door that reverberated loudly throughout the otherwise quiet interior of Rachel's cloistered in—law apartment!

THREE:
ERRAND
OF
MERCY

"Heaven and earth are enduring. The reason why heaven and earth can be enduring is that they do not give themselves life. Hence they are able to be long—lived.
Therefore the sage puts his person last and it comes first,
Treats it as extraneous to himself and it is preserved.
It is not because he is without thought of self that he is able to accomplish his private ends?"
—Lao Tzu, Tao Te Ching, Book One, VII

We looked across at each other, contemplating each other's faces worriedly.

"It sounds like somebody with a purpose," I remarked.

"I'll answer it," I offered, getting to my feet first. "Let me go see who it is."

"No, Francesco," Rachel objected demurely, standing up. "It's my house. I live here."

"Fair enough," I relented, "but I'll go with you."

She parted her pretty lips to object again but I cut her short.

"I won't intrude," I assured her, throwing up my hands resignedly, "I promise."

Together, we walked straight to the front door through the in–law's narrow, carpeted hallway. I stood on one side as Rachel cautiously cracked the door open.

"Excuse me, ma'am," I overheard the familiar, raspy voice of the very familiar cop announcing himself, "my name's Dave Toski—homicide inspector for the San Francisco police department."

"As I live and breathe," I scoffed, heaving a heavy sigh of relief as I stepped up to the doorstep alongside Rachel to confront the craggy–faced cop still holding up his flipped–open identification badge.

Rachel abruptly came at me, pressing both of her palms fast against my chest.

"I'm so very sorry, my Francesco," she said, frantic, lifting up her pleading eyes to meet mine, "I did not betray your trust to call the police, please believe me! I did not mean for you to lose face—*mien tzu!*"

"What are you talking about?" I asked her, grasping her gently by the arms, rubbing them reassuringly. "It's all right, Rachel, I know this character. He's a dubious friend of mine. So don't worry, all right? I'll talk to him, all right?"

She moved back, bowing her head, nodding.

"You're frightening the lady," I told Toski, peeved, running my eyes over his familiar, tall and lanky six–foot–four frame decked out in that familiar, rumpled tweed, herringbone sportcoat patched at the elbows. "What do you want? I'm on retreat."

"Not anymore you're not," Toski contradicted me with a shake of his head. "And I'm not alone. Nolan's here with me. Even Bennie."

"Hey, Frank!" Nolan Quinn, proprietor of the *Buena Vista Cafe*, betrayed himself from behind, his familiar big, brawny, pale, freckled, red–haired visage in view.

"Frank!" my chubby and cheerful cabbie buddy, Bennie Brennan, waved his hand, bringing up the rear.

"What the hell is this?" I hissed. "A visit from All–the–Usual–Irish–Suspects–Committee?"

"Can we come in for a minute, Frank?" Toski asked.

"It's not up to me," I told him, gesturing to Rachel. "She's the lady of the house."

"Can they come in for a minute?" I asked, turning to Rachel for her reply. She bowed her head, nodding.

"Okay," I said, gesturing invitingly for the intruding trio to enter the in–law's foyer. "You can come in for *just* a minute. But we're busy and we're not entertaining guests today."

So the intruding trio all filed in together, looking a little jittery.

"The gang's all here then," I volunteered to do the introductions, gesturing first to Rachel. "Gentlemen, this is my guardian angel, *Shih*-Tseng, so treat her nicely."

Rachel smiled knowingly at my emphatic—and correct—pronunciation of her name.

"*Shih*," I continued, gesturing to the other three, "now about these reprobates: this is Dave Toski, SFPD homicide inspector extraordinaire; Nolan Quinn, my main

48

benefactor and landlord; and last but not least, Bennie Brennan, my private Uber–Lyft driver all rolled into one! And how's Beverly?"

"She's still the rock, Frank," Nolan said. "She's holding down the fort back at the cafe. We're both hoping you'd consider coming home. We've been really worried about you. And when I got the call—"

"Beverly is Nolan's lovely wife and right–hand woman," I clarified for Rachel. "What call?"

"Miss Chung here called your emergency contact number," Nolan explained, "that's me, of course."

"You silly girl!" I said, warmly enfolding Rachel in my arms. "So that's what you were so worried about. No need. You did nothing wrong. Besides, I owe you my life."

"Well, gentlemen," I continued, turning to confront the intruding trio once more, "I thank you all for your concern, but if that's all, we won't detain you any further."

"I'm sorry, Frank," Dave Toski apologized, "but this isn't a social call. And I'm afraid I'm going to have to detain *you* a bit further."

"What the hell's this all about?" I snapped.

"I need you both to come down to the Central Station on Vallejo Street to file reports and make statements."

"What the hell for?"

"About last night's little incident in the alley."

"Oh, that!" I said. "Forget that! That's all water under the bridge by this time. No real harm's done—thanks to my angel here. And besides, I don't want to get her involved in anything."

"She's already involved, Frank—you both are," Toski insisted. "And that gash on your chest says some major injury was done. We'd like you to get that attended to first thing, by the way, at the Chinese hospital since it's closest."

"I'd forgotten all about that, surprisingly," I said,

palming my sore, bandaged chest through my shirt. "Why can't we just forget the rest of it, too?"

"We just can't, Frank," Toski said solemnly. "I'm afraid it's much more serious than even that."

"Serious? Serious how?" I asked, conspicuously concerned.

"It's your gun, Frank."

"My gun? What about it?"

"You lost it."

"Those hoods that attacked me took it."

"We've recovered it."

"So you've recovered it. So what?"

"Not before it was used in the commission of a crime, Frank."

"Crime? What kind of crime?"

"A serious crime, Frank," Toski said gravely. "A very serious crime."

"You should've posted that picture of *Chung Kuei* at the door *before* these characters came," I quipped halfheartedly, turning to look knowingly at Rachel, smiling weakly at her.

"Pardon, Frank?" Toski asked.

"Private joke, Dave," I answered. "Let's go."

§

Chinese Hospital
845 Jackson Street
Chinatown

Chinese Hospital hovers high six stories, buttressed by massive rectangular columns, as a stately, slaty gray, concrete building with polished marble interiors on Jackson at Stone Street, another extremely slender alleyway that crosses it. I sat, reclined comfortably on a slender bed—covered, curiously, in black instead of white—in the cream–colored recovery room of the hospital's first–floor emergency room department. Rachel sat beside me in a swivel chair, very regardful of my condition.

"I'm all patched up," I reassured her lightheartedly. "Not that many stitches so it wasn't as bad as it looked. And the quack complimented the professional quality of your Band–Aid!"

"I'm glad," she said, conspicuously still upset. "You could've been killed."

"But I wasn't—thanks to you. So forget it. It's all over and done with."

"I went to temple to pray for you today," she told me unexpectedly.

"So that's where you went when you were out earlier," I said, surprised. "A *Joss House*?"

"Yes."

"I thought it was mostly a showpiece for tourists these days."

"Not for the devout who still believe."

"You're a believer?"

"*Sun Yat–sen* was a Christian," Rachel conceded with a slight jest. "Still, there is no race so successfully resistant to outside influence as the Chinese. It is difficult to define a *Joss House* to an honorable Occidental such as yourself."

"Try me."

"A *Joss House*," she elucidated, "is not a church, a mosque, or even a conventional temple though it can retain elements of all three. It is not a thing of sect or doctrine. It is simply a…place of worship. Into it is emptied all of the faiths and influences the Chinese have absorbed and adapted over centuries of their civilization. It may embrace symbols of a pagan past—with its engaging gods of forest and stream, field and farm. It may incorporate symbols of venerable ancestor worship—the philosophies of Confucius and Lao—tsze or the religion of Buddha."

"The derivation of the term, *Joss House*," she went on, "signifies its broad purpose. The word, *Joss*, is a corruption of the Portuguese word, *deos*, meaning God, and goes back to the days when Portugal was one of the few countries trading with China. It is a House of God, then, with no confining limits as to any special manifestation of His presence."

"So there's no one god housed in a *Joss House*?"

"Conceivably," she told me, "there are as many gods to worship and supplicate as there are causes. And goddesses, too. Today I went to invoke on your behalf, *Wah—Taw*, the God of Medicine."

"That was most thoughtful of you," I told her, smiling mirthfully.

"Yes," she continued, "I went to the *Tin How* in Waverly Place, which of course is named in honor of the Chinese Queen of Heaven. Being without dogma, creed, or congregation, you go to the *Joss House* on personal errands, so to speak. To be as near heaven as possible, all *Joss Houses* hold forth on the topmost floor of any building which harbors them."

"Then the *Tin How* was the perfect place for an angel to frequent," I said, taking one of Rachel's delicate and tapering hands warmly in mine.

§

That was when Dave Toski, SFPD Inspector 73, rudely interrupted us with his abrupt entrance into the room.

"I've dealt with all the paperwork and red tape," he told me, "so you're all ready to be discharged. You were really very lucky last night, Frank."

"Thanks a lot, Dave," I said, smiling knowingly at Rachel, "but I had the god, *Wah—Taw*, on my side."

"If you say so," Toski sniggered. "We've got this serious matter to discuss, briefly for now—your license could be on the line."

"You can speak freely. I have no secrets from my guardian angel here. So what's the deal with those hoods? I thought hatchet men were phantoms of the past."

"Were that the case. There's modern—day highbinders operating, all right. But nowadays they're usually gang members hired by mobsters to do their dirty work for them."

"Modern—day *boo how doy*! Wonders never cease. So, this serious matter?"

"We found a young Chinese girl shot to death in **Cooper Alley**. We found your gun on the ground next to her."

"*My* gun?"

"It was thrown down by the body in defiance like a gauntlet—in true highbinder style. It was wiped clean."

"Naturally."

"Ballistic's yet to determine for certain whether it's the actual murder weapon. But the victim's a suspected prostitute—the name of *Kum Quai*."

"That's horrible—"

"No!" Rachel blurted out before anyone could say anything more, gnashing her teeth into both of her upraised clenched fists. "It just can't be!"

She just as abruptly burst into tears, crying convulsively—and uncontrollably.

FOUR:

ASSIGNMENT: CHINATOWN

"The spirit of the valley never dies.
This is called the mysterious female.
The gateway of the mysterious female
Is called the root of heaven and earth.
Dimly visible, it seems as if it were there,
Yet use will never drain it."
—Lao Tzu, Tao Te Ching, Book One, VI

FRANCESCO FERRARI
EXPLORES CHINATOWN

LILY POND
GOLDEN GATE PARK
SAN FRANCISCO, CA

Lily **Pond**, its marshy surface with floating water lilies nowadays overgrown by spreading duckweed, was once an idyllic, crystal–clear reflecting pond with a clay–lined bottom in its sequestered spot on that short trail off John F. Kennedy Drive in **Golden Gate Park**; where I'd pulled up my gun–metal gray *Ferrari California T*, parking at the roadside across from the **Conservatory of Flowers**, the park's majestic glass–wood–and–masonry Victorian greenhouse with its 60–foot–tall pavilion rising in the distance. Surrounded by Australian tree ferns, Rachel and I thread our way together along the narrow, meandering north–south footpath that girdles the pond, which was once an old chert rock quarry, its tranquil boundaries demarcated by brown, white–lettered signs set atop tall, metal poles: **Lily Pond**. We came up to a little wooden bench to sit down on.

"Thank you for bringing me here, Francesco" she told me.

"I wanted you to feel better," I said, half–smiling. "How can you know for sure that this girl—*Kum Quai*—is the same one you know?"

"Chinatown's a tight–knit community of maybe only 20 square blocks, but it's a living, breathing community where residents are closely connected. And *Kum Quai* is no prostitute. She's a young Christian girl—and no *rice Christian*, either. She's also a waitress at the same restaurant where I work and, like me, she's also a struggling student."

"Rice Christian?"

"Converts who embrace Christianity to enjoy material benefits, basically."

"Instead of having a true spiritual conversion, you mean?"

"Yes. And rumor–mongering is rampant in Chinatown. Right above the restaurant where we work is a massage parlor called the *Darling Dragon*. A young masseuse named *Choy Cum*—who is a known prostitute—has recently gone missing from the parlor. She calls herself *Selina* for her clients. She just left without a trace—and nobody knows where she is—as if she's gone into hiding."

"What makes you think the cops would confuse the two girls?"

"Come now, Francesco, most Occidentals can't tell different Orientals apart."

"If that's the case, *Kum Quai*'s student visa status could easily be verified."

"It is the case, Francesco," Rachel affirmed. "we commiserated a lot about our situation."

"Your situation?"

"Yes," she explained. "We have a highly competitive education system in Taiwan with an elaborate examination structure—similar to that of imperial China! Starting at a very early age, we are taught that our future depends on our ability to pass examinations and get into good schools. To succeed, you have to study hard. The pressure for achievement is so intense that failure brings shame to the whole family. We are taught English in junior high school because the goal is to go to the United States to earn a graduate degree. Taiwan tailors its curriculum to the American system, so that graduates can easily adjust to American graduate schools."

"It sounds like your country trains its students for export," I commented.

"Exactly—its *best* students, that is."

"Of which you are one."

"Perhaps. Except—"

"Except?"

"The system encourages us to specialize in technical fields in demand in the American job market. So the best students are pushed by their parents and teachers into computer science, engineering, medicine—even if we're more talented or interested in the humanities or social sciences. Even those of us who major in business tend to concentrate on the more technical aspects, such as accounting or corporate taxation."

"And which is your particular focus?"

"I came here to study accounting."

"But your heart really isn't in it?"

"You can hear my heart crying, can't you, Francesco?"

"I think so, yes," I said feelingly.

"I'm constantly fighting myself by fooling everybody else, but I can no longer fool myself."

"How do you mean?"

"Chinese parents tend to project their intense ambitions onto their children. Good grades in school and entering a first–rate college are encouraged not only by the family but by relatives and even family friends. There's this constant pressure and supervision of the young to develop discipline—and to internalize their parental values as their own. So we grow up with a high regard for hard work and accomplishment. That's why I work hard to succeed at accounting and pretend that I enjoy doing it."

"I always thought there was a traditional reverence for learning amongst the Chinese—that the Chinese have a deep respect for knowledge because of their Confucian cultural background."

"The current reality is that the Chinese pursue higher education for very practical reasons—like concentrating on fields in which we're most likely to get good jobs. Chinese families emphasize education. Taiwan's elite raise their children to settle permanently in the United States.

They do not bring up their children to become American prostitutes. And *Kum Quai*'s family is part of that elite that came from mainland China to dominate Taiwan's politics."

"If what you say is true," I said with a shrug, "then this whole thing could be a very tragic case of mistaken identity."

"All right, Francesco, I give in," Rachel said, abruptly changing the subject. "I'm dying to know what this gift you brought to give me is."

"Oh, *that!*" I teased, deliberately caressing the lengthy package lying on my lap tied with a red–bowed ribbon.

"It's just a small token of my gratitude and appreciation for everything you did for me," I told her, handing it over to her.

"I'm so curious," she exclaimed, unwrapping the package gingerly, "the suspense is killing me!"

Rachel peeled the paper to lay open the package with care—with an expectant gasp!

Gradually exposed to view was the whitish, glazed and glossy porcelain figure of a genuine antique *China Doll*—some 30–plus inches tall—with painted, molded hair and facial features!

"And that's how you see me, is it?" she asked, her eyes immediately moist.

"China Doll's actually a misnomer as the true antique is *German*–made and hard to find as this one was," I told her, trying to make light of the emotional moment. "But, yes, I see its beauty and rarity in you—both inside and out."

We warmly embraced, enfolding ourselves in each other's arms, crimping the doll between us—Rachel's pretty almond eyes spilling with soft tears that wet my shoulder where she'd buried her face.

"Thank you!" she whiffled in my ear, holding me tight.

FRANCESCO FERRARI
EXPLORES CHINATOWN

"Francesco," she started gently once she moved away to lift up those penetrating eyes to rivet on mine, "I wish to ask a great favor of you—with all humility."

"Anything, anytime," I told her unhesitatingly but with a decided frown, looking befuddled, "you know that."

Then she sprung it on me quite simply.

"I want to take you to meet *Kum Quai*'s parents—in Chinatown!" she said.

§

Apartment
Second Floor
Jackson Street
800 Block
Chinatown

Chinatown is a city within a city and was once home to the greatest concentration of Chinese sojourning outside of their homeland. Not a single inch of this small urban maze has been wasted by its people, who have lived virtually on top of one another in basements, cellars, courts, dormitories, garrets, lofts, and porches. That district's narrow streets have remained crowded, sometimes dirty, noisy, and smoky, and have been lined instead of gold with brick–and–wooden tenements—sometimes fetid firetraps—overrunning with humanity. Impoverished conditions, and the necessity of keeping close within Chinatown's boundaries—mainly to avoid violent confrontations with white society in times past—created this residential overcrowding. Housing has always been at a premium so sojourners had to bear with these cramped quarters. Poverty makes their overcrowding inevitable.

These Chinese have occupied every inescapable crack and cranny of Chinatown. They have been trained by centuries of stifling sociality. They like crowds, clamor—and

61

jostling elbows. Ten bunks in a room eight–by–twelve has sometimes been their notion of social contact.

This familiarity with crowded living makes the Chinese masters of arrangement. Give any Chinese a green pepper, a couple of freshly laid eggs, and a half–dozen oranges, and those will instinctively fashion a picture as they're laid out on the kitchen table. If they empty a tub of salt fish and put it out on the back balcony, and toss a ragged rice sack of matting and two discarded ginger jars beside it, you will see a perfect study in still–life. These Chinese have been constrained to conserve funds, time—and space. Ordinary people in such situations stifle beauty. But the Chinese are *extra*ordinary people. They treasure beauty and if they cannot indulge their taste for art with Ming vases, they create art intuitively out of ordinary staples of life—food, fragments, even refuse.

No tenement in Chinatown has been too squalid to lack at any window a potted plant or two—stunted and often flowerless shrubs somehow filled by mysterious touches with esoteric character. Glimpses of those back balconies discover a clarity of line and detail: a broom leaning against a wall, an abandoned bamboo tub, the shallow basket brimming with drying squid—all fall into place to make that picture.

This apartment located within this battered, three-story building painted a faded olive green with windows trimmed in chipped maroon—in sight of **Chinese Hospital**—was no different: scrim curtains draped those windows and raised shades betrayed the overstuffed furniture.

In one corner of the room stood a solemn *family altar* carved from teakwood tables, set with pewter incense jars surmounted by Buddha lions, and ceremonial candles dyed a deep vermilion with trappings of gilt–and–silver paper made into fabulous butterflies. Lily bulbs shot up fragrantly scented blossoms of cream and gold, platters of mandarin oranges, mounds of yellow cumquats, arranged upon the table with an uncanny sense of composition. Astonishing bouquets of paper flowers, combining countless colors and forms, arose from pink–and–green vases and were transformed by some sorcery into perfect beauty and symmetry.

It boasted an additional *shrine*—a gilded tablet engraved with black symbols. A triangular cluster of artificial blossoms surmounted with peacock feathers crowned the tablet. Drapings of turkey–red cotton cloth hung on either side. Before this shrine rested oblong tin containers filled with sand into which were thrust *joss* or incense sticks—*xiangbang*—for making burnt offerings.

Placed in front of that shrine was an ornate, figural-style funerary—or burial—*urn* with a customary cover and narrow neck above a rounded body with a footed pedestal. I was told that it contained the cremated ashes of Rachel's fellow worker friend, *Kum Quai.*

Kum Quai's elderly parents sat close together on their overstuffed sofa, their hands tightly clasped atop the husband's knee. Their timeworn, wrinkled faces displayed a tragic lifetime of indescribable but unspoken hardship, pain, suffering, and misery. They lifted up their pleading eyes to me and I stood before them, abashed and bewildered.

"This is *Ming Long* and *Chun Fah*." Rachel told me, introducing me to them, translating for us our back–and–forth exchange of words as we all talked together.

"How do you do?" I nodded, smiling half–heartedly.

"We want to crave a great favor of you," the father started doubtfully, "because we are told that you are a great detective."

I glanced over at Rachel, looking perplexed.

"Our daughter was a good, hard–working Christian girl," the father went on, his voice breaking even in Cantonese. "She was not a prostitute—could never be a prostitute. It would be much—too much—to ever expect you to ever find out who killed our beautiful, young, and innocent little daughter: *Kum Quai*. But we do ask you—we *beg* of you—to please help us to clear the good name of our daughter, *Kum Quai*, and to prove to the police that she was not a prostitute. And we are willing to pay you any price for you to do this for our *Kum Quai*."

I suddenly stood aghast, openmouthed and speechless.

"I'm sorry," I said shakily, almost incoherent, "I apologize. I am highly honored by your confidence in my ability—but I feel most unworthy of it and must most respectfully decline to accept a request that I could never accomplish."

After Rachel's last translation, both of *Kum Quai*'s parents bowed their heads, folding their hands prayerfully, squeezing shut their moistened eyes as they both nodded emphatically in the affirmative!

"What did you tell them?" I asked Rachel, confounded.

"What you said," she repeated sedately, "that you were very moved by their confidence in your ability and—"

"And what?" I hissed.

"And," she added as a nonchalant afterthought, "that you would try to do your very best to fulfill their touching request—and not to be concerned with any cost for your help."

I promptly shrank—bodily—moving back to plunk myself down in an overstuffed armchair, shaking my head as I buried my face in my hand in utter disbelief; smearing in my warm palm the tears welling out of eyes forced into hiding. Rachel stepped up to me quietly, gently touching my shoulder with her delicate, outstretched hand.

"*Nga ega tin ne do ahma*," she whispered to me, expressively, with all her heart. "I give you the heavens for courage, my Francesco."

FIVE:

BRANNAN STRET WHARF ONWARD

*"Without stirring abroad
One can know the whole world;
Without looking out of the window
One can see the way of heaven.
The further one goes
The less one knows.
Therefore the sage knows without having to stir,
Identifies without having to see,
Accomplishes without having to act."*
—Lao Tzu, Tao Te Ching, Book Two, XLVII

FRANCESCO FERRARI
EXPLORES CHINATOWN

Red's Java House
Pier 30
South Beach
Embarcadero

Red's Java House is an elongated, cream–colored wooden shack of a dive diner, supported by concrete pilings, stretched out into San Francisco Bay off the eastern *Embarcadero* waterfront roadway in sight of the western section of the gray steel truss, double–deck, double–suspension *Bay Bridge*. Its twin front windows trimmed in maroon, its white–painted front door hung open as an open invitation to patrons, its familiar, angled, white, rooftop sign lettered in red endures as its bayfront beacon: *Red's JAVA HOUSE!*

If I was going to try to do this thing at all, I figured that I ought to at least make the effort to try doing it right by getting into some semblance of decent physical shape: so I sported my navy blue sweat suit and *Asics* running shoes and wheezed my way through a strenuous jog–trot along the breezy, wind–swept pedestrian promenade— dodging in and out of the crowded and rambling procession of other joggers, walkers, and cyclists on my way.

I was en route to a rendezvous with a reputable Sunday columnist for the *San Francisco Chronicle* newspaper, who was noted in particular for his extensive knowledge of the city's history. And this case I was sucked—or rather, suck*ered*—into looked like it could involve sex trafficking: a line of inquiry I'd never had occasion to follow before. So I figured getting the historical lowdown on this subject of controversy could be useful.

Getting to the diner, I stepped inside, setting foot on its wood–plank flooring, and picked my way past rectangular metal tables with battered, red–vinyl stools, passing through the narrower, rearmost section lined with a row of smaller, square wooden tables and chairs placed by picture windows looking out on placid, sea green waters. Going out the rearmost exit to the diner's expansive outdoor deck, I promptly spotted the columnist—recognizing him instantly from his newspaper photo—sitting, relaxed, in a metal chair at a lone, cream–colored table. He was nursing a *Paddy* blended Irish whiskey from the full bar installed at the diner's cement patio.

He was a venerable, square–jawed gentleman, wearing a rumpled gray suit with a carnation tie and spectacles— balding and bearded, but not doddering; graying but not wrinkled. His ear lobes were long, his cheeks cherubic, his nose prodigious; his mouth was wide and thin–lipped, his eyes decidedly discerning and intelligent.

"Hello," I greeted him, stepping up to his table, my hand extended. "I'm Frank Ferrari."

"Carl Dolte," he said, squeezing my hand.

"*Dolt*? You're kidding me."

"It's Dolte—with an *e*!"

"Oh," I chuckled. "Sorry."

"Don't be. It's a genuine surname—however unflattering. Can I buy you a drink?"

"I'd love to, but no thanks, I'm on the wagon—so to speak."

"I understand. I've been there."

"So," I started, sitting down after he gestured to the chair across from him, "you're a *Chronicle* columnist."

"I write the Sunday *Native Son* column."

"I can't say I've ever read it. But I have heard the *western song*."

"What's *that*?"

"The miners came in forty–nine," I recited jauntily, "the whores in fifty–one, and when they got together..."

"They made a *Native Son!*" we recited together—in

unison—laughing aloud!

"So, Mister Ferrari," Carl Dolte suggested, "you're something of a historian yourself?"

"Strictly amateur class," I admitted. "That's why I've come to you as you have this expert reputation."

"I'm more of a historical veteran by virtue of age," he said modestly. "So, you're looking for a link between sex trafficking history in San Francisco's Chinatown and a *contemporary* case you're working on, currently?"

"The past informs the present—or so I gather."

"Yes, well," Carl Dolte said sardonically, "the first thing to understand, historically, is that no such thing as sex trafficking ever existed in Chinatown as such—strictly speaking, of course."

"Never existed?" I asked, aghast.

"No," he declared assertively, "something far worse and much more malevolent—much more depraved—persisted in Chinatown: sex *slavery*!"

"Sex slavery?"

"You probably presume, erroneously," Dolte started, "that slavery in this country was effectively abolished with Lincoln's Emancipation Proclamation. Yet there existed for years—on this Pacific coast—a slavery so vile and degrading that all the horrors of negro slavery could not even begin to compare with it!"

"How so?"

"Long after blacks were freed in these United States," he elaborated, "*mal*practices involving Chinese women were tolerated in California and elsewhere in the American West that were, in essence, human bondage. A decade after the Thirteenth Amendment abolished black slavery, outlawing even involuntary servitude, this *other* slavery— this trafficking of young Chinese women—was flourishing in San Francisco and throughout the West. And because Chinatown was in the original core of the city, this brazen trade in human flesh was taking place just a few blocks away from both the city's financial district and its most exclusive neighborhood: *Nob Hill*. So far from being a thing of the past, human beings were being bought and sold into a far worse slavery than Uncle Tom ever knew of!"

"That's some pretty strong stuff you're telling me."

"The point being," he emphasized, "if ever there was slavery, *this* was slavery right here in our own city! And it's a good thing you put on your running shoes."

"Why's that?"

"Because," he confided to me urgently, "we've got a lot of walking to do. Come on!"

§

"It all started with a major influx of Chinese—Chinese males in particular—that came to America in two waves," Carl Dolte recounted as we strolled southward along the breezy *Embarcadero*. "The California gold rush during the late 1840s brought the first wave to dig for gold in the Sierra foothills. Once the rich surface gold mines were exhausted, most white miners moved on to more productive sites. Only big mining companies had the required capital to work underground, and to earn a fair return, they needed a reliable supply of cheap labor. So *coolies*—which means bitter labor in Chinese—were brought to America from southern China as contract labor.

"Once gold mining began to decline in the late 1850s, this demand for cheap labor shifted to railroad construction. Then came the second wave of Chinese—to finish the most difficult section of the transcontinental railroad in the Rockies. And in the 1860s, China provided *thousands* of railway workers for the construction of the *Central Pacific Railroad*. They labored under harsh and dangerous conditions as they swung pickaxes to connect California to the eastern seaboard.

"Once the railroads were finished, Chinese were need-ed to help develop other western industries. They built levees, hauled away mud to dig irrigation ditches, and re-claimed marshlands for the delta farmlands of the Sacra-mento and San Joaquin river valleys—some of the most productive agricultural regions in the country. They were employed in salmon canneries in Alaska—and on the Columbia River in Puget Sound. They worked in textile mills and small–scale factories—making gunpowder, pro-ducing silk, rolling cigars, sewing garments."

"Calling the Chinese *industrious* would be an under-statement then," I noted.

"Quite," Dolte agreed with a nod. "So Chinatowns were established in the 1880s—first in the major metropolitan areas on the west coast and, later on, New York, Philadel-phia, Boston, Chicago, and other cities. This shift of Chi-nese into these urban ghettos was involuntary. These were segregated areas where the Chinese were forced to stay."

"Why was that?"

"To exclude the Chinese from the larger labor market, of course."

"Of course."

"These Chinese ghettos differed from their European immigrant counterparts in one very significant respect: the near total absence of families."

"*Women*, you mean."

"Right. When the first Chinese coolies came to Amer-ica, precious few women accompanied their husbands, so women were extremely scarce. As a result, the Chinese male–to–female ratio was heavily *skewed*."

"Where did that *coolie* moniker come from?" I asked him, interrupting his discourse.

"The word *k'u–li*," he explained, "derives from the Tamil—Indian—and is often translated as hard or bitter strength. It refers to the resolve required for a laborer to sell himself into that kind of indentured servitude—called the contract–labor system—which was really something akin to slavery. Unlike the traditional coolie slave, though, Chinese immigrants to America, however humble, were their own men."

"So gold was their reason for leaving China?"

"Gold—the lure of it and the hope of riches from it—was enough to send them across the ocean into an unknown world. They left their villages, their families, and everything that was precious and dear to them—with the dream of finding wealth on the fabulous *Gum Sam*, or Golden Mountain, as they called California. First hundreds, soon thousands, and then tens of thousands of Chinese peasants would sail for here. It was a massive migration of the sojourning *gum saan haak* in search of the supposed riches of the *Gum Saan*."

"The gold rush and the Chinamen are only part of the story, I take it."

"You take it right," Dolte affirmed. "If there had not been a gold rush in California in the nineteenth century, thousands of Chinese peasants would've had no reason to brave the Pacific crossing—and *girls*, in poor villages in China, might've never been sold by their starving families to supply the burgeoning sex slave trade in the American west!"

"The heart of the matter, as it were," I suggested.

"Or the *vitals* of the matter, whichever you prefer," Dolte declared. "Denied conjugal relations, many solitary Chinese males idled away their leisure and led the lives of homeless men. Bereft of family life, and deprived of female companionship, these men resorted to prostitutes to seek pleasure and intimacy."

"The prostitutes providing not so much companionship as a sexual outlet for lonely men—performing a biological function to satisfy their pent–up sexual appetites."

"Still," Dolte qualified, "these Chinese were bound by traditional customs not to plant roots in the devils' country. Though separated by many mountains and vast seas, they were required to return to their homeland to fulfill their filial obligations and preserve their family ties. After all, *Confucius* once said: *while father and mother are alive, a good son does not wander far afield.* And there are no older or stronger family, clan, or homeland ties on the face of the earth than those in Chinese society!"

"By the 1860s," Dolte recounted, concluding his precocious discourse, "the trickle of emigrants from China to San Francisco turned into a torrent. And as America's biggest city west of the Mississippi, San Francisco boasted the single greatest concentration of Chinese residents in the country. Those who trekked here in the nineteenth century called it *Dai Fou*—or Big City!"

"So," I surmised, heaving a heavy sigh, "where their countrymen dared to venture their prostitutes dared to follow."

"Precisely," Dolte affirmed. "And here's roughly where they disembarked—before, that is, being taken to a place nearby most euphemistically called the, *Oriental Warehouse!*"

Just then, we were approaching the **Brannan Street Wharf Waterfront Park**.

ever, Chinese sojourners immigrating to the American west in the nineteenth century were not slaves. They traveled of their own free will and they paid their own way. Their emigration to California was free and voluntary."

"*Un*like the prostitutes who followed them here..."

"Chinese girls were destined for another sort of life in *Golden Mountain* altogether," Dolte said seriously, "these poor raft–and–boat–born women of Canton landed here like so many blocks of wood. These were sex slaves—peasant girls and mostly teenagers—likewise from the Pearl River delta—bought in China for small sums of money and bound for San Francisco to be sold in Chinatown."

"*Bought* in China?"

"Like so many cases of tea," Dolte said in a caustic tone, "they were bought on order in China and brought to this country. Here they were sold to the highest bidder—some being sold as wives or concubines to rich Chinamen, mostly wealthy merchants—but most of them sold into the custody of the proprietors of the so–called houses of ill–fame."

"Bought from whom?"

"Their parents, guardians, or owners—at sums varying from thirty to two–hundred dollars each, according to their age, personal appearance, and accomplishments. Younger, stronger girls were preferred, of course. Fourteen–year–olds were considered the perfect age for prostitution. These girls would often work as house servants or grow up in brothels before being forced to sell their bodies. Whatever price a girl fetched in China, she could be worth ten, twenty, or even thirty times as much in *Golden Mountain*."

"These girls were sold by their own *families*?"

"Routinely," Dolte said sedately. "Peasants sold girls during times of crushing hardship—often their youngest child—to the highest bidder."

"How could they do that?"

"Prostitution was a profitable solution for relieving families of their female members. And her sale, or part of her earnings, could help support the family. In times of war or natural disaster, families often resorted to the selling of their children for whom they couldn't provide."

"Then again," Dolte added, "many believed they'd sold their children as brides or concubines for Chinese men in America—or else as indentured domestic servants called *mooi–tsai*—a Cantonese term meaning *little sister*. These girls worked as domestic servants in San Francisco while young but were often sold into prostitution once they were older. For parents, these exchanges were pivotal to the family's survival—to forestall penury."

"Why would families care to *relieve* themselves of their females?"

"Because girls were considered dispensable," Dolte explained. "In the male–dominated, patriarchal Chinese family, daughters were sold more often and with less reluctance than sons. The teachings of Confucianism place far more value on sons than on daughters. As the Chinese proverb says: *a boy is born facing in—a girl is born facing out! Goods on which one loses,* was the phrase that most parents attached to their daughters. That's why they were bought and sold like chattels."

"So I suppose it's safe to say that an army of prostitutes followed this army of Chinese laborers entering America?"

"Such an influx of males in great numbers without family restraints is *always* followed by prostitution," Dolte emphasized. "Armies breed cosmic urges and loose women to gratify them. And the substitute for decent female companionship was the substitute that's been put in place since time immemorial: *in*decent female companionship!"

"And this," Dolte concluded, gesturing dramatically

to the calm bayside embankment in front of us, "is roughly where that army of Chinese sex slaves first landed in San Francisco!"

§

Intersection
Brannan & Delancey Streets

"For a good forty years," Carl Dolte reflected thoughtfully as we crossed the **Embarcadero**, and bent our steps westward, strolling between rows of low–roofed, modern but prefabricated looking buildings on that quiet, two–lane, tree–lined portion of Brannan Street, "and even beyond that, these Chinese sojourners thought of themselves as living in a transient world. They stood with the left foot on the western shore and the right foot still planted squarely on the shores of their forefathers. Their wives, their children, their ancestral altars all remained in the Far East. They never thought of the new world as even fit to receive their bones."

There we stood in sight of the soaring, 1070–foot **Salesforce Tower** skyscraper, shimmering in the distance down Delancey Street.

"How were these prostitutes lured here?" I asked.

"Pro*cured* is the word," Dolte corrected me. "By false promises and enticements meant to tempt and entrap, mostly, the baits being: education, employment, gold, marriage, money—you name it. Girls difficult to recruit could be broken down—drugged, raped, confined—until their spirit was broken and they accepted the inescapable: prostitution. Another of their luring methods was straightforward, forcible seduction. Sometimes they were outright abducted or kidnapped. Professional procurers—slave brokers, really—were nicknamed *white ants*."

"Nothing's changed then. Today, I've heard, the very

SEVEN:

QUEEN'S ROOM TO HOSPITAL

"*A man is supple and weak when living, but hard and stiff when dead. Grass and trees are pliant and fragile when living, but dried and shrivelled when dead. Thus the hard and the strong are the comrades of death; the supple and weak are the comrades of life.*
Therefore a weapon that is strong will not vanquish;
A tree that is strong will suffer the axe.
The strong and big takes the lower position,
The supple and weak takes the higher position."
—Lao Tzu, Tao Te Ching, Book Two, LXXVI

FRANCESCO FERRARI
EXPLORES CHINATOWN

Dick Lee Pastry
716 Jackson Street
Chinatown

Parklets, so–called, or penned–in sidewalk tables, were becoming all the rage in this city—even in Chinatown. In this instance: a pair of little cream–colored, picnic–style tables with matching blue benches, decorated with a lone yellow–potted, blossoming plant, where we sat together outside, sipping on a couple of Thai iced teas. Underfoot was spread a maroon rug.

Overhead, yellow, red–lettered banner signs blazoned:

Dick Lee Pastry, All You Can Eat Dim Sum: $5.99

Established in 1978, and owned by Peter Yu, also known as *Dick Lee*, this long–time dim sum shop specializes in a variety of savory dishes: barbecued pork bun, golden pan–fried bun, dumplings, spring rolls, fried noodles, hand–pulled, no–oil noodles, clay–pot rice, fried rice, porridge, brocolli beef, chicken feet, sesame chicken, roast duck, and siu Mai. It occupies the first floor of a weathered, three–story, olive green building. Tragically, we weren't there to partake of the flavorful food. Quite the contrary, we were there to discuss *barracoons*.

We sat in sight of one of Chinatown's narrowest alleyways—**St. Louis Alley**—whose slim mouth opened out to Jackson Street. Directly across the street from the dim sum shop, it cut its spare passage through two three–story brick buildings.

"The next destination for these hapless Chinese prostitutes was the so–called *Queen's Room*," Carl Dolte solemnly recounted, "most *in*aptly named."

"Why inapt?" I asked.

"Because," Dolte explained, "the bitter irony was: there was nothing whatever royal about the *Queen's*

"Not quite," Carl Dolte said gravely, "as we've yet to pay a visit to the final destination of many a Chinese prostitute—the Chinatown *hospital*!"

§

COOPER ALLEY
CHINATOWN

Not far from Kearny Street, running parallel through three—story buildings, the extremely constricted throat of **Cooper Alley** opens out to Jackson Street as it cuts its extremely narrow passage southward—just six feet across—through the rising brownstone walls on either side. Low—lying metal fire escapes, hovering above, cast the slate—colored asphalt into darksome and somber shadow. Squeezing through this extremely slender alleyway felt cramped and confined.

"Of course," Carl Dolte related, "prostitution regularly employed young women whose prime years were between fifteen and thirty. After thirty, prostitutes had to seek alternate employment. With the ravages of time—and the loss of their youth and beauty—prostitutes also faced the loss of their occupation."

"That stands to reason," I observed, "tragic as it is."

"What you can't possibly conceive or imagine," he told me fatefully, "is what became of these broken or trampled blossoms—as they came to be called—if they fell ill and lost their ability to attract customers. If they took sick, they could be turned out into the street and find no relief except in the most agonizing death. Such prostitutes were left alone to die in dismal little rooms—without light, bedding, or clothing—which were dumpheaps most euphemistically called...*hospitals*!"

"What were they afflicted with the most?"

"They contracted venereal diseases, of course, or came down with ailments induced by drug abuse, the infirmities of older age, or any number of other physical disorders," Dolte recounted. "Few had the means to seek medical treatment. City health authorities, reflecting the anti–Chinese mood of the nineteenth century, often shut them out from medical facilities. Physicians in San Francisco once lobbied to ban Chinese prostitutes from the City and County Hospital. Their owners outright refused to provide them with any nursing care once they could no longer work—and could no longer serve their purpose of bringing in money to their masters and mistresses. So they'd be discarded—cast aside to die miserably in any corner without any relief of their suffering. Tragically, these most gravely ill of Chinese prostitutes faced death alone."

"And those so–called hospitals?"

"Those consisted of little more than small, damp, foul–smelling dens furnished with straw mats and dimly lighted by a China nut–oil lamp," Dolte related. "Let's pay a brief visit to one of those *hospitals*, shall we?"

§

We came to a miserable padlocked door not more than five feet high. Dolte unbarred it and budged it open, grinding on its rusted hinges. It opened into a room some nine feet in length and not so wide. On one side was a ramshackle shelf four feet in width and a yard above the filthy floor, upon which were spread a pair of long–rotted rice mats. There was no trace of any furniture—no table, chairs, or stools—nor any window through which some stray stream of sunlight could be thrown upon the room. Its atmosphere was close and clammy—deathlike and permeated with the vapors of ancient disease and disorder.

"To this place," Dolte recounted, "were brought those

girls who became so infected by disease that they were no longer money–making machines and became burdens to the slave–masters who owned them. And here these wretched creatures, deserted by humanity, with no one to turn to for help, ended their miserable lives.

"When any of these unfortunates was no longer useful, and a Chinese physician passed the opinion that her disease was incurable, she was notified that she must die. Led by night to this hole, she was forced through the door and made to lie down upon the shelf. A cup of water, another of boiled rice, and a little metal oil lamp were placed by her side. Her murderers went out of the death cell, the heavy door was locked, and the unfortunates were left to die alone. What agonies those poor victims must've suffered in their lingering deaths can't be conceived. The smothered scream of despair, the moans and groans of their torment, were totally ignored and neglected.

"After several days the lamp burnt out, the faint light failed for lack of oil, the rice and water cups went empty and dry, and the joss–sticks which were lighted when the girl was brought to the cell were nothing but charred splinters of bamboo.

"Invariably, the girl was dead—either by starvation or by her own hand. Sometimes if life was not extinct, and some spark yet remained, she was left again until her heart ceased to beat and her breath stopped. She was considered worthless waste."

Stopped dead in my tracks, I swallowed hard, feeling choked and sick to my stomach.

"And this town has the gall to pretend that it's so fucking enlightened," I said scornfully, full of contempt, "terminally bragging about that so–called San Francisco spirit—and being the city that knows how. Yeah, it knows, all right. It knows *shit!*"

"For too many," Dolte declared, "suicide became the

94

quick solution to their despair. The worst part was: when death came, their remains, unlike those of most Chinese emigrants, were seldom sent back to China. Chinese custom obliged relatives to pay the fare for bodies to be shipped back to China. But if nobody was willing to pay for transportation back to China, the corpses were simply dumped in the city's streets and alleys."

"If you have any leftover doubt whatever that this was nothing more or less than full–scale sex slavery," Dolte told me in parting, pulling out some folded papers from his jacket pocket, "then I'll leave you with these, Mr. Ferrari."

"What's this?" I asked, taking from him the papers he gingerly handed over to me.

Intently, I inspected the papers—which turned out to be photocopies of certain authenticated historical documents.

"*Bills of sale*," Carl Dolte told me sober–mindedly, "paper contracts and agreements stipulating the specific terms and obligations attached to the physical sale and purchase of several actual Chinese prostitutes of the period—like so much salable merchandise. These were the goods and commodities in the trade of human flesh—and blood!"

EIGHT:

A LILAC OF A MASSEUSE

*"The strategists have a saying,
I dare not play the host but play the guest,
I dare not advance an inch but retreat a foot instead.
This is known as marching forward when there is no road,
Rolling up one's sleeves when there is no arm,
Dragging one's adversary by force when there is no adversary,
And taking up arms when there are no arms.
There is no disaster greater than taking on an enemy too easily. So doing nearly cost me my treasure. Thus of two sides raising arms against each other, it is the one that is sorrow–stricken that wins."*
—Lao Tzu, Tao Te Ching, Book Two, LXIX

FRANCESCO FERRARI
EXPLORES CHINATOWN

Chinatown of old endures, and survives, as a quarter of fabulous fantasy and legend: a flickering gas—jet dying out in the lurid gloom of a stairway; a gaudy lady with seed pearls in her hair making a shadowy display upon a balcony; the burst of six—shooters spurting murder and sudden death in a blind alley are provocative obscurities that wreck havoc even with strict realists. Set the stage dimly and let dark figures skulk across it and there are precious few spines that can withstand the tingle. This Chinatown—that—was had this gift of somber mystery. Its daylights only half-heartedly betrayed its realities, but its nights were mysterious with otherworldly shadows that bred fantastic myths and fanciful tales.

Chinatown of old was a district that had been built by Boston traders, abandoned, and handed over to a people who painted lintels and window frames orange, red, and sky—blue as their fancy dictated; who daubed their brick walls with scarlet and pitch—black posters. They hung fish to dry from the rooftops, they filled their wrought—iron balconies with porcelain flower pots and bellying lanterns, they sprouted lily bulbs by the hundreds upon their fire escapes. Daybreak would irradiate the banners and lanterns dangling from those brightly painted balconies. Visually, though, the *Oriental* note was still a shallow veneer.

In some cramped alley, a wanderer chanced upon a doorway smeared with yellow, crimson, or blue that led upwards into a damp darkness; where it was only human to expect something fantastic at the end of a shadowy passageway; where anything could happen to an intruder who stepped from the cheery daubing of the entry into a heavy gloom made all the more ominous by the fitful flickerings of a pale lamp upon the lower landing.

That wanderer might find himself in a forbidden corridor leading to an illicit gambling club; or amidst the sweetly sickening fumes of an opium den; or in a bagnio occupied by twittering slave girls; or he might stumble upon a secret tribunal of a highbinder tong marking a man for death! It was depravity itself draped in dismal gloom—plagued with those gambling parlors, opium dens, and brothels—and populated by slave girls, Chinese gangsters known as highbinders, and terrifying professional assassins called hatchet men!

But that brightly daubed doorway, smothered so completely in provocative gloom, might just as easily have led to a faithful wife stirring the rice–pot over a charcoal brazier; or a young musician plucking shrill notes from a moon fiddle; or an aged philosopher reading the precepts of Confucius through his horn–rimmed spectacles.

Even its pungent odors were distinctive and unmistakable: being a blend of burning joss–sticks, nut–oil, and straw–matting. This was all long before the incursion of its countless curio emporiums and shops, peddling everything from firecrackers to foo dogs, and chop suey restaurants serving dried abalone and salted plums.

§

You deep in–denial, revisionist historians will most persistently avoid admitting that the feverish flames of the earthquake–and–fire of 1906 licked up a pretty foul old Chinatown quarter. Bubonic plague had infested its fetid confines for many a long day, and the day its residents had absconded before the purging sheets of fire, a vast and mighty army of loathsome rats absconded with them. Once the beleaguered city began to look forward, the dreaded question presented itself: what disposition to make of the Chinese! Everybody appeared agreed that they would never be permitted back at the old site.

A committee on *Securing a Site for Chinatown* was convened that went about searching for desirable locations—ultimately selecting one someplace to the south amidst mud flats. To the south of the city, **Hunter's Point** created a cove where tiny but delectable shrimps abounded. One of the first pursuits of the Chinese in San Francisco was fishing for those shrimps. They kept a monopoly on that pursuit and their one–time settlement on the south shore was as old as any Chinese settlement in California.

With their customary serenity, the Chinese uttered nothing, offering neither proposition nor opposition, but they went on record in no uncertain terms: they would either return to their old quarter or else. They were accustomed to the cobblestone slopes of Clay and Sacramento Streets. They'd been there since the very start.

New Chinatown started very unornamentally. It was slab–sided and functional. Part of the Chinese genius, though, is making the most of necessity, and soon *exotic* touches started betraying themselves: fire escapes transformed themselves into balconies and window ledges converted into fragmentary gardens. At first, they contented themselves with a shop or two along Dupont Street. Very gradually, they scaled the heights, taking over the two–story dwelling–places that could not remain secure from the placid penetration of the Far East.

For a while, the Chinese quarter looked like it was doomed to perpetual drabness—condemned to being a colorless section of cream–colored brick—the pageant of an alien and foreign skyline yet to be born. Then one day an *American* public service corporation set up a telephone exchange that could've been a Chinese pavilion. Fantastic cornices, a forest of gilded turrets, and pagoda tops hung with bells all followed suit—as did bazaars, food shops, and even tong quarters. Along the street of bazaars known as Grant Avenue, lamp–posts supporting dragons bracing miniature pagodas, glimmering with amber lights, replaced their banal American counterparts. Even as an empty shell, the quarter assumed the outward appearance of the *Orient*!

Out of the ashes and rubble of that cataclysmic earthquake sprang up—like the fabled Phoenix—the new *Oriental* City: influenced by *Look Tin Eli*, a California–born merchant who had founded one of Chinatown's biggest tourist–oriented businesses, the **Sing Chong Bazaar**. Look, who was secretary of the **Chinese Chamber of Commerce**, convinced other entrepreneurs and property owners that they could attract more tourists by rebuilding Chinatown in an *Oriental* Style. But it was the *American* architecture firm of **T. Patterson Ross and A.W. Burgren** that designed numerous fine and handsome buildings, including Look's, in *Oriental* style—many with multi–story, pagoda–like roofs. Though the steel–framed top of the **Sing Chong Bazaar** was purely ornamental, this commercial temple was lit up at night by thousands of incandescent bulbs to intentionally create a sense of *Oriental* enchantment.

Historian *Philip P. Choy* called the phenomenon a pseudo–*Oriental* style, taking Chinese elements like the pagoda's curved eaves and wrought–iron balconies ornamented with the Chinese double–happiness motif, converting new structures into something unique using *American* materials and methods. Even the San Francisco *Real Estate Board* commended the rebuilt Chinatown as picturesque and tourist–friendly. Tiny lights and the exuberant use of the Chinese colors of green, red, and yellow turned a dark and crowded ghetto into what one architectural digest called the *Fantasy of the Far East*.

At Grant Avenue and California Street, catty–cornered to Old Saint Mary's church, structures were constructed at a cost of $135,000 and leased to the **Sing Fat Company**. At 32 Spofford Alley, *Charles M. Rousseau* designed a new $25,000 home for the **Chinese Society of Free Masons**, the

Chee Kong Tong, with a great deal of *Oriental* detail and Chinese tile.

Money motivated this convenient revival of China-town in the end. Occidental property owners in the area recognized the great value of the rents they'd been paid by their Chinese tenants. Together, then, Chinese and white landowners established the *Dupont Street Improvement Club*—named after Chinatown's main thoroughfare. Numerous real estate investors—pillars of the business community—made their fortunes directly from prostitution.

If you're still in deep denial about Chinatown's special *Oriental* nature, in light of facts and reality, then you've been robotically programmed beyond all free, independent, and rational thought.

§

Some uninformed or mis–informed contemporary commentators claim, falsely, that Chinatown covers some 20–square blocks in area nowadays. In reality, though, Chinatown's true inner core—her true sectional heart and soul—has remained unchanged since the late nineteenth to the early twentieth century!

Granted, Chinatown's dense population has long since spilled over the old boundaries of Broadway, California, Kearny, and Stockton Streets—but the quarter's heart is the same *dozen* blocks as of old. She's even bled over, yes, the western confines of Powell Street, losing herself amidst modern flats and still more modern apartment houses.

San Francisco's earliest Chinatown, the ghetto of roughly *eight* square blocks, was still north America's largest and oldest Chinese settlement. By the late 1800s, there were thousands of Chinese people living in the city, packed mostly into the *eight*–square–block area bordered by Sacramento, Stockton, Kearny, and Pacific Streets. After the earthquake of 1906, Chinatown expanded her central borders to *twelve* square blocks. That was when Sacramento was known as *T'ang Yen Gai*—or *Chinese Men's Street!*

I was there to home in on just one destination on just one of those streets amidst the larger maze of Chinatown.

§

Darling Dragon Massage Parlor
Second–Floor Building
Jackson Street
Chinatown

Darling Dragon Massage was situated, just as Rachel told me, atop the very restaurant where she worked with the somewhat archaic name, **Peking Garden.** Signs posted at the massage parlor, featuring portraits of beautiful and seductive young Chinese models, titillated the prospective customer with suggestive turns of phrases like: *very friendly* masseuses and *tender touch* massages—hinting that this could be a place that would rub you up the *right* way!

Atop the short flight of carpeted steps, smelling of lemongrass, I was greeted at an upright, marble–topped reception desk—bearing a tall, potted, periwinkle plant—by a matronly, stern–faced Chinese woman who broke her frowning expression with a mannered smile. She promptly held aside a flowery, gossamer curtain hanging from the ceiling, opening up a short, cream–colored hallway with black baseboards. Underfoot, I scuffed across the thick, gray carpet. On either side, the walls were framed with latched doors trimmed in black.

"We have six private rooms for massage," she told me, leading me to a secluded back room.

"Pick your girl, sir," she invited me, gesturing to four Chinese girls slouching on a sizable sofa—all very young, very soft, very fresh, very demure in demeanor, and very scantily–clad.

"Do any of these young ladies speak English?" I asked, running my appreciative eyes over them.

"All my girls speak very excellent English!" the matron boasted.

"I was hoping for *Lilac Chen*," I said suggestively. "I've heard she's very good."

"Enjoy your massage, sir," the matron bid me as the one called *Lilac Chen* coyly led me to one of the small, spare, and surprisingly spotless private rooms.

There was a slender bed with padded headrests draped in white and piled with hot, peach–colored towels. *Lilac Chen* set out bottled lotions and oils on a tray table nearby.

"Is this your first massage?" she asked me.

"Here," I answered.

"You like *special* massage?" she asked, lowering her voice to a soft tone.

"What do you mean?" I asked, playing dumb.

"For a good tip," she quickly clarified, gesturing for me to sit down on the mattress, "we can make sex."

She warmly palmed my inner thighs, fingering her way to my crotch.

"Wait just a minute," I objected, gently clenching her wrists. "I want to talk to you first."

"Talk?" she asked, looking disapproving and perplexed.

"To get to know you a little better."

"I do not understand," she shook her head, confused.

"My name's Francesco," I told her. "What's your name?"

"I am Lilac Chen."

"No, I mean your real name—your Chinese name."

"Why do you ask me that?" she asked, slightly timid.

"Tell me, please, I just want to know."

"*Sieu Cum*," she said shyly.

"Listen to me, *Sieu*," I told her softly but urgently as I bent close to her. "I'm looking for *Choy Cum*—the girl who calls herself *Selina*. She could be in a lot of trouble. I need to find her. I want to help her."

"No!" she shook her head worriedly. "I should not say anything about this!"

"*Sieu*," I insisted, slightly tightening my clutch, "please believe me. Choy could get hurt—and very badly—if I do not find her first. I only want to help her. You must trust me!"

"I do not know anything," she said nervously, just as insistent. "I cannot tell you anything."

"*Sieu*," I demanded softly, "look at me!"

I stared at her intently until she lifted up her pretty, almond eyes to meet mine.

"*Choy* could be in very great danger if you do not tell me," I said as sincerely as I could. "I only want to help protect her to stop anything bad from happening to her! I beg you to trust me, *Sieu!*"

"I think," *Sieu* said, relenting reluctantly, "I think *Choy* go mission! She go mission! That is all I know."

"She go mission?" I said, confounded. "You mean the Mission district?"

Then we were very rudely interrupted as three men burst abruptly into the little room unannounced—two brawny, robustly–built white toughs, crowding side by side a slender, younger Chinaman, sporting that traditional black *changshan* tunic—again!

"We would very much like to know the reason why you are so interested in locating our *Selina*," the Chinaman said stoically, addressing me directly.

"And we would very much like you to tell us that reason—right now," he added with a decidedly menacing tone of voice.

NINE: FALLING IN LOVE

"Truthful words are not beautiful; beautiful words are not truthful. Good words are not persuasive; persuasive words are not good. He who knows has no wide learning; he who has wide learning does not know.

The sage does not hoard.

Having bestowed all he has on others, he has yet more;

Having given all he has to others, he is richer still.

The way of heaven benefits and does not harm; the way of the sage is bountiful and does not contend."

—Lao Tzu, Tao Te Ching, Book Two, LXXXI

FRANCESCO FERRARI
EXPLORES CHINATOWN

Darling Dragon Massage Parlor
Second-Floor Building
Jackson Street
Chinatown

One of those Occidental toughs promptly man-handled the young girl called *Lilac Chen* out of the room.

"Take it easy with the lady," I protested.

And the other Occidental tough stiff-armed me with his outstretched palm pressed firmly against my chest. I glowered at him.

"What the hell is this?" I objected. "This is supposed to be a private party!"

"The party's over when you start to worry our workers, as it were," the young Chinaman volunteered, stepping up to me.

"Who are you then? And what do you want?"

"My name is *Kai Ming*," he told me, introducing himself. "I'm a protector of this establishment."

"A protection racketeer, you mean?" I said, sarcastic, eyeing his pair of white toughs. "What about *Mutt and Jeff* here?"

"Meet Hunter and Murray," he said, gesturing to them. "They're my trusty bodyguards."

"Bodyguards?" I cracked with a chuckle. "That's a switch—the Occidentals guarding the Orientals! I didn't know Chinatown was such a rough area."

"It can be in certain quarters," Kai Ming conceded. "Hiring white bodyguards was the start of a vogue among *highbinders* of old. Any hatchet man would think twice before gunning down a white man to get at his Chinese enemy. If he did, he could have a lynch mob of *fan kwei* after him. The killing of whites would most definitely mean the end of the casual attitude of the white Establishment,

109

which tolerates the crime that thrives in Chinatown. White bodyguards for the *Mandarins,* as we once came to be called, became quite a fad. I'm simply following the fashion of my honorable ancestors."

"You must be joking. Are you telling me you're a mod-ern—day highbinder?"

"I'm not telling you anything. You're telling me, Mis-ter—"

Those two toughs pilfered my pockets to pluck out my identification wallet, handing it over to the Chinaman.

"Ferrari," he finished. "Are you a cop, Mister Ferrari?"

"Private," I readily admitted, "but I'm not working— ask anybody. I haven't been working for weeks, months maybe. I've been drinking so much lately that I've lost track."

"Then why the intense interest in locating our Selina?"

"I heard she provided a great...*service,* is all."

"From whom?"

"From someone who would prefer to remain name-less...on account of their marital status."

"I see. Then you're claiming that you're not here to do any...detective work?"

"That's a laugh. I doubt that I'm even capable of doing any *detective* work anymore."

"What then was the cause of this supposed incapac-ity?"

"I don't care to talk about that," I answered, adamant.

"I'm not inclined to believe you, I'm afraid, Mister Ferrari."

"I don't give a flying fuck what you believe. Lookit, I came here strictly for recreational purposes. All I know is—because you barged in here with your *Bobbsey Twins,* I didn't get my nuts off as anticipated!"

"Then I suspect that we'll just have to take you at your word—this time."

"And next time?"

"Next time," Kai Ming stated ominously, "I cannot promise you anything. As a matter of fact, you are as safe anyplace here in Chinatown as you would be in your own back yard."

"If I had a back yard," I cracked.

"We Chinese have humor enough never to molest Occidentals as a rule."

"That's very sporting of you."

"Every rule has its exception, however, Mister Ferrari," Kai Ming added forebodingly. "And we might not be so *sporting* the next time! Leave now. And never come back."

Resignedly, I held up my hands, and slipping past those two strapping white toughs, I vacated that massage parlor as quickly and as quietly as I could!

§

Rachel's In-Law
Ross Alley
Chinatown

I'm ready for my close-up, Mister DeMille!

Yes, think that celebrated American film director of epic scope and cinematic showmanship: *Cecil B. DeMille!*

Every now and again, during my rather promiscuous sexual career, I'll come across that female lover—yes, *lover*, not corporate "partner"—who wrongly presumes herself in bed to be the *Cecil B. DeMille* Director of Lovemaking. Communication, she insists, is key to satisfying sex and fulfilling lovemaking. So she'll proceed to literally and most meticulously direct your every move—ordering precisely which sexual button to push, which knob to turn, and which lever to pull! The ever predictable result:

the most *unnaturally* forced, mechanical, and machinelike lovemaking imaginable.

Rest well–assured, ladies: you don't *talk* love—you *do* love! And most importantly, as Rachel would remind me with just two simple words, you *feel* love!

§

"I really blew it at the massage parlor, I'm afraid," I confessed abashedly to Rachel over mincemeat, noodles, and Chinese tea. "I'm sorry."

"You still came away with a lead," she said, trying to pacify me.

"That mission bit?" I hissed. "It doesn't mean anything that I can figure. And if *Sieu* did happen to mean *the* Mission—that's just another quagmire of a district to get bogged down searching in. Believe me, I know."

"I have confidence in you, Francesco, even if you have none in yourself."

"You're a very lovely girl, Rachel," I told her feelingly, "and I owe you more than my life. But I'm frankly very sorry that you ever roped me into this thing. I just don't feel right running all around Chinatown—like some *Great White Hope*—trying to solve something that's probably unsolvable."

"I'm not a girl as you keep calling me, Francesco, and I wish you'd stop."

"You're not?"

"No."

"How old are you?"

"Twenty–four."

"I rest my case," I chuckled.

"What difference does age make?"

"It doesn't—some people are mature far beyond their years. Others are infantile for their age."

FRANCESCO FERRARI
EXPLORES CHINATOWN

"So what are you saying?"

"I'm saying *revel* in your youth and *revel* in being a girl while it lasts—instead of lamenting it!" I told her pointedly. "Live your life and savor the experience! You'll be a full–grown, grown–up *woman* soon enough! Once you reach forty–four—then come back and tell me how much you miss being a *girl* again!"

"I was right, my Francesco," she told me, laughing aloud, "you really are an antique!"

"But like the all–seeing, all–knowing sage," I joked, "I'm wise well beyond my years!"

"Which reminds me," Rachel said as if suddenly remembering something, "speaking of things antique!"

She got up abruptly and went over to her bunk bed, plunking herself down on the mattress—patting it as a marked gesture, inviting me to join her sitting there. With a slight shrug, I got to my feet to do just that.

In the wicker chair nearby, Rachel had propped up the glazed porcelain **China Doll** I'd given her in its own silent and stoical sitting position. Next to her bed, she'd set up her laptop computer atop that nightstand in place of the books she'd stacked there before.

"I wanted you to hear one of my all–time favorite songs," she told me, "sung by the artist who performed it the best."

Surprisingly as ever, Rachel played for me the black–and–white television *YouTube* video she'd saved of the late, great singer–jazz pianist–and–actor, **Nat King Cole**, poignantly performing the popular standard, written in 1952 by Victor Young and Edward Heyman: **When I Fall In Love**!

When I fall in love
It will be forever
Or I'll never fall in love
In a restless world

113

Like this is
Love is ended before it's begun
And too many moonlight kisses
Seem to cool in the warmth of the sun
When I give my heart
It will be completely
Or I'll never give my heart
And the moment I can feel that
You feel that way too
Is when
I fall in love
With you

Once the song—a moving romantic love ballad—concluded, Rachel bowed her head and demurely folded her hands in her lap, staying still and silent.

"That's a very loving song," I said, gently.

"Maybe I'm in a loving mood, Francesco," she said without looking up.

All Rachel had on was a flimsy, satiny soft silk gown, which just then fell open at the top, exposing to tantalizing view the fleshy curve of her smooth and supple bosom.

"I hate to sound salacious,"I said, slightly suggestive, "but it looks like you're not wearing anything underneath that gown."

"I'm not."

"Is that...an invitation?"

"No," she said, turning to me to lift up her eyes, welling out just enough to glisten. "It's a desire to know something I've never known before."

"Never?"

"Never."

Slowly, I reached out to take her cheek in my palm—already warm and moist to the touch—letting my hand leisurely fall, softly caressing her sleek neck, sliding down to part her top and gently fondle her velvety soft breast as

I bent to kiss her mouth, just as gently exploring her lush lips.

Those two words she paused—a little breathless—to softly tell me:

"Be tender."

TEN:

DECONSTRUCTING THE POLITICALLY CORRECT

"My words are very easy to understand and very easy to put into practice, yet no one in the world can understand them or put them into practice.

Words have an ancestor and affairs have a sovereign.

It is because people are ignorant that they fail to understand me.

Those who understand me are few;

Therefore the sage, while clad in homespun, conceals on his person a priceless piece of jade."

—Lao Tzu, Tao Te Ching, Book Two, LXX

FRANCESCO FERRARI
EXPLORES CHINATOWN

This time, it was my turn to leave a little note behind for Rachel to read once she woke up before I slipped quietly out of her in—law apartment. I left her whiffling softly in her sleep— looking so peaceful and prepossessing in repose:

> *Rachel,*
> *I've gone to follow up that lead.*
> *I've saved a YouTube video for you to play.*
> *Please listen to it with love in your heart.*
> *Francesco*

I wasn't there to watch her stir languidly in her bed, awaken, sit up and, slightly sluggish, shift herself to play the video I'd saved for her to see—or the warm, expressive smile it brought to her flushed face: popular singer—songwriter *Johnny Mathis* performing the love ballad—**You Are Beautiful**—from the 1958 Rodgers and Hammerstein musical, **Flower Drum Song**, based on its celebrated namesake novel by the Chinese writer, *Chin Yang Lee*:

> *You are beautiful, small and shy.*
> *You are the girl whose eyes met mine*
> *Just as your boat sailed by.*
> *This I know of you, nothing more,*
> *You are the girl whose eyes met mine*
> *Passing the river shore.*
> *You are the girl whose laugh I heard,*
> *Silver and soft and bright;*
> *Soft as the fall of lotus leaves*
> *Brushing the air of night.*
> *While your flower boat sailed away,*
> *Gently your eyes looked back on mine,*
> *Clearly you heard me say,*
> *You are the girl I will love some day.*

To this day, unbelievably, there are those who terminally complain about this wonderful musical adaptation of *C.Y. Lee*'s equally wonderful novel, whining childishly and clamorously about how *offensive* to them the story is supposed to be—as if the whole wide universe revolved around none but them and their petty, self–conscious, and hyper–pretentious little sensibilities—and was supposed to automatically(and unrealistically)conform to their warped, self–superior, and artificially contrived politically correct outlook.

Well, I was headed for a contentious confrontation in Chinatown with one of these extremist fanatic conformists who was long overdue for getting dealt a potent dose of real–world reality!

§

Chinatown Community Development Center
1525 Grant Avenue
Chinatown

Chinese society stands on a literary pedestal. Mastering the language of China is a remarkable feat of memory. There are fifty–five thousand ideographs in all! Ideographs possess a pictorial content apart from their form. They suggest a word picture to those who understand. A man's position in China is said to be measured by the extent of his mastery of the language.

Even the spoken word is no mean feat. Their language consists of three hundred and thirty monosyllables—each of which, in turn, has four different sounds that convey different ideas.

Chinese lettering, though, is a term that's a misnomer. Chinese *characters* are something more than mere lettering—they are word *pictures* composed with a beauty of line that makes them partake of both the literary and pictorial arts. Many a Chinatown sign possesses this beauty of line.

Protruding from the cream–colored, first–floor facade

to the gray, three–story building on Grant Avenue, the small black sign with little white letters, hanging over the community development center's double–maroon doors, looked pretty nondescript. Its chubby Chinese director, *Malcolm Yang*, sporting the stubble of a five o'clock shadow and wearing a rumpled, ill–fitting suit, looked equally undistinguished—eloquent though he was at articulating his politically correct doctrine.

"Carl Dolte over at the *Chronicle* referred me to you," I explained after Malcolm Yang gestured for me to sit down across from his desk in his office. "I was hoping—with your familiarity with the community—that you could give me some insight into Chinatown's core identity—what really makes the quarter tick."

"Not being seen as a model minority," he preached like a reflex reaction. "The Chinese are making it and doing well because we stick together. We're willing to start at the bottom and help one another rise and get ahead."

"I don't get that," I admitted. "Being industrious and enterprising are admirable qualities but you're disgruntled by that perception."

"This perception grossly simplifies reality."

"So, what? You aspire to be assimilated so much that you prefer being perceived as dysfunctional and screwed up as your white counterparts?"

"Basically," Yang expounded with a dismissive chuckle, "Chinese today break down into two distinct groups— the more professional *uptown* Chinese and the less professional *downtown* Chinese, for want of better terms.

"*Uptown* Chinese, either American–born or new immigrants, have more education and higher incomes. They don't live in concentrated ethnic communities. Because they arrive with professional skills, they're better equipped to integrate into American society, so they don't settle in Chinatowns."

"They don't have to start from scratch, so to speak," I offered.

"On the other hand," Yang continued, "a great many Chinese are new, low–skilled immigrants who speak little English, who work at low wages in dead–end jobs as manual and service workers—like waiters and seamstresses. They come from humble origins, traditionally from the rural areas of southern China, so their relatives are likely to have similar backgrounds. They comprise the *downtown* Chinese—and tend to settle in Chinatowns with their sponsoring relatives. Chinatowns like San Francisco's are bursting at the seams with these *downtown* Chinese."

"So most Chinatown residents are working–class?"

"And their plight isn't pleasant," he affirmed with a nod. "They work overlong hours a week with no overtime, no sick, retirement, or vacation pay, no health benefits, and no job security. Chinatown families live in run–down, three–room railroad flats—frequently with three generations living together."

"They're just surviving and trying to get by like everybody else."

"Everybody else isn't forced to work in an *underground economy*," he said contrarily.

"Underground economy?"

"An economy not protected by American labor law," he clarified. "where factory owners dodge social security payments, landlords charge key money, Chinese bank owners ignore banking regulations, youth gangs extort protection money from shop owners, and tongs intimidate—even murder—dissenters."

"And American labor laws don't apply?"

"Businesses operate regularly with two sets of books to under–report income and evade taxes. Their workers and suppliers are paid off the books. Workers aren't expected to report their income, either. They routinely ignore fair labor practices."

"None of this sounds very...*legal*. Why doesn't anybody pitch a bitch about it?"

"Nobody dares to complain," Yang told me. "Chinatown is still controlled and dominated by a traditional political elite which rules with the acquiescence of outside authorities. This structure was transplanted from feudal China during the nineteenth century. Clan associations and secret societies—like the celebrated *Six Companies*—were first set up to arbitrate on behalf of the Chinese. They were first known as *huiguan*. Once established, though, these mutual–aid fraternities developed a power of their own. They came to rule the working people in Chinese communities. This traditional order continues to exist today even though it's been modified. It's adapted to modern conditions to serve a new class of landlords and owners in Chinatown. It's an informal political structure but it keeps a firm grip on the destiny of many a Chinese in this country."

"What's the attraction to Chinatowns then?"

"For Far East investors and employers," Yang answered, "it's the ample supply of cheap immigrant labor they provide, obviously. Their working conditions are extremely exploitative. This exploitation is heavily disguised when Chinese work for Chinese employers."

"How's that?"

"Due to the hands–off attitude of American officials who mostly do not intervene in the internal affairs of ethnic enclaves. And being unwilling to talk to outsiders, most residents are reluctant to project a negative image of the community for fear of retaliation—or for reasons stemming from ethnic pride."

"How extensive is this...exploitation?"

"There's an old Chinese saying, Mister Ferrari," Yang recited, "*for the fame of one general, ten thousand corpses are left on the battlefield*! Being poorly paid, unable to speak English, uninsured—and unlikely to be unionized—these *downtown* immigrants are the last to be hired and the first to be fired."

"If standard labor practices are being ignored," I suggested, "then you're indicting the Chinese for exploiting the Chinese."

"Correct," Yang conceded. "The central premise for this underground economy in Chinatown is cheap labor. Waiters and shop clerks are expected to work six days a week, more than ten hours a day—with no compensation for overtime, no holidays, and no sick leaves. They're paid below the minimum wage. In large and busy restaurants, waiters don't even receive wages—their income consists entirely of tips. And most have to chip in two–thirtieths of their tips to management to divvy up among the other staff."

"This sounds more like *slave* labor than cheap labor," I said, scornful.

"In a very real sense it is," Yang asserted. "It's a corrupt system sustained by Chinatown's informal political structure—with the tacit consent of outside government officials."

"That seems to dispel the idealistic notion of solidarity amongst the oppressed."

Yang shrugged, nodding.

"As fascinating as this class–struggle discussion is," I digressed, "I was hoping to make more of a connection to *sex* slavery than to slave labor."

"For all that," Yang concluded, "Chinatown endures as an active immigrant gateway for low–income newcomers to this country—and provides a source of starter jobs for these new immigrants."

"Is this center involved in any efforts to counteract this so–called underground economy?"

"Not directly," Yang confessed. "We're collaborating with other organizations to create a new cultural center intended to slow displacement and gentrification in Chinatown. This new center would feature contemporary exhibitions to spark discourse about pertinent issues of the day—like global warming, domestic violence, and racial injustice."

"Issues of the day?" I sniggered derisively. "That's going to be of mesmerizing interest to Chinese workers slaving away for starvation wages and seventy–hour workweeks! Discourse about global warming should leave them utterly spellbound!"

"There's no need to be facetious."

"It just seems to me that maybe some good, old–fashioned, activist labor organizing might be more in order."

"Just what do you care about the Chinese, Mister Ferrari?"

"The *Chinese*?" I repeated, fully fed up from the exhaustive fatigue suffered from listening to Yang's long-winded and debilitating dissertation. "I don't give a damn about the *Chinese*!"

"I thought not."

"No!" I told *him*. "You don't *think*! At all! That's just the trouble. You spout witless platitudes. You parrot the phony propaganda of the PC party line—like some mindless puppet. It will probably come as a great shock to you: but the whole wide world really doesn't revolve around your trivial, ethno–centric fixations! The very *last* thing you ever do is *think*!"

"That's enough," Yang sighed tiresomely.

"What I care about is helping people in trouble!" I persisted. "*People*—as in members of the human race! You know, *Homo sapiens*—the same species we both belong to! And right now there's a young girl somewhere in Chinatown who could be in a great deal of trouble—whose life could be in danger if I don't find her before some very nasty hoodlums do! And she happens to be *Chinese*!"

"What is it that you want to know?"

"What does it mean for a young girl in Chinatown—a runaway prostitute in particular—to go to *mission*?"

"For a former Franciscan seminarian such as yourself, Mister Ferrari," Yang chortled contemptuously, "that should've been extremely simple for even you to figure out by now!"

"Oh, my God!" I muttered to myself—the clear–cut revelation dawning on me ever so suddenly.

"I'm sorry," I apologized, getting abruptly to my feet to go.

"For what?"

"Not for what I said," I clarified. "I'm sorry that people like you simply can't be reached. I'm sorry that your supreme shallowness is so—"

"*What?*"

"*Self–inflicted*! Thanks for the tip."

At that, I turned on my heel and promptly left.

ELEVEN: CAMERON MISSION AND BEYOND

"Thirty spokes
Share one hub.
Adapt the nothing therein to the purpose in hand,
and you will have the use of the cart. Knead clay in
order to make a vessel. Adapt the nothing therein to
the purpose in hand, and you will have the use of the
vessel. Cut our doors and windows in order to make
a room. Adapt the nothing therein to the purpose in
hand, and you will have the use of the room.
Thus what we gain is Something, yet it is by virtue of
Nothing that this can be put to use."
—Lao Tzu, Tao Te Ching, Book One, XI

FRANCESCO FERRARI
EXPLORES CHINATOWN

Donaldina Cameron House
920 Sacramento Street
Chinatown

Malcolm Yang was right about one thing though: I should've known right away what *mission* meant!

Chinese members of the *demimonde*—disreputable women—historically took refuge in Methodist and Presbyterian rescue homes run by women missionaries. These rescue homes were offshoots of prevailing missionary work in San Francisco. Though the Presbyterians were the first in the city to establish a specifically *Chinese* Mission—in 1853—they lagged behind the Methodists in the development of a rescue home providing care for criminal, homeless, and wayward girls and women. In 1870, the Methodists opened their **Mission House** in their *Chinese* Mission building on Washington Street. Presbyterians in 1874, by contrast, opened their **Mission Home**, operating from cramped rented quarters; shortly thereafter, they relocated to a twenty–five–room tenement on Sacramento Street. Chinese brothel residents fled to either refuge when owners abused or mistreated them.

These missions demonstrated a rudimentary understanding of the root causes of prostitution by providing haven for prostitutes, teaching them new trades and finding them employment—sewing shirts, shoes, undergarments and otherwise toiling in the city's major sweatshop industries of the day: boots and shoes; cigars and tobacco; sewing; woolens. Until the mid–1880s, school lessons taught by missionary school–teachers comprised the only formal education available to Chinese women living in San Francisco.

Chinese prostitutes became the favored objects of mission charities. During the 1880s and 1890s, it was the era of rescue missions and settlement houses—a time when Christian charity demanded deeds, not words.

One of the most successful charitable organizations working with Chinese prostitutes was the **Occidental Board of the San Francisco YWCA**. In 1881, under the board's auspices, a home was founded to shelter Chinese girls rescued from the brothels. After 1896, the home's director was gentle but resolute *Donaldina Cameron*, also known as the *Jane Addams of the West*. For forty years, rescue work under grim Cameron consisted of raiding Chinese brothels where young prostitutes were forced to stay against their will. By 1925, the last slave–girl raids were made in *Portola Alley*—renamed *Cameron Alley*; renamed *Old Chinatown Lane*.

§

"The Home," *Kelsey Pak*, **Cameron House**'s charming young communications coordinator described the stocky, square structure constructed of dark, irregularly cast clinker bricks to me, "was originally built on a narrow lot just eighty feet wide and one hundred thirty–seven–and–a–half feet deep. It was a two–story, brick *Dutch Colonial* building. Though it was demolished by the 1906 earthquake, it was rebuilt at the very same site and—as you see—still stands today."

"Impressive," I observed. "*Donaldina Cameron* was a truly extraordinary woman."

"She took pride in the Home's showpiece—the *Oriental* Room," Pak recounted, "a grand parlor furnished with Chinese carpets, rugs, Cantonese hangings on the walls, green silk curtains, porcelain vases, and tables inlaid with mother–of–pearl. In the dark corners of its basement, a runaway girl could hide out behind sacks of rice or underneath shelves near the gas meter. The scent of Chinese food would drift throughout the entire house."

"Intriguing," I said, "but I gather that you're no longer providing safe haven for escaped prostitutes as in times past."

"Nowadays," she informed me with a slight shake of her head, "we perform a far–ranging variety of community services such as adult education, cancer support, community resources, counseling, domestic violence case management and support groups—even food distribution."

"All that's remarkably admirable," I complimented her, "but what I seriously and urgently need to know is this: if a Chinatown prostitute turned up on your doorstep today seeking shelter—where inside Chinatown could she be referred to?"

"Is this a hypothetical question," she asked, eyeing me suspiciously, "or are you inquiring about someone in particular?"

"A little of both," I readily admitted. "I'm looking specifically for a young Chinese girl named *Choy Cum*. Her life could be in grave danger if I don't find her before some other people—who could be a threat to her—do. It's a long shot, of course, but there's a possibility she could've come to **Cameron House** seeking safe refuge. If she had, I thought you might've referred her to another safe house."

"I see. Well, due to privacy and security concerns, I couldn't comment on any individual's specific case—"

"Naturally not."

"But…"

"But?"

"Given your respectable reputation," she carefully qualified herself, "I could reply to your query, hypothetically speaking, by recommending that you check out the **Gum Moon's Women's Residence** on Washington Street— and inquire further there."

Grinning broadly, I squeezed Kelsey Pak's hand

warmly.

"Thank you," I told her, breathing a gratified sigh of relief. "Thank you."

§

Gum Moon Women's Residence
940 Washington Street
Chinatown

In 1868, Reverend Otis T. Gibson founded the **Methodist Mission**, also known as the *Oriental* **Home and School**, located at 916 Washington Street in San Francisco's Chinatown, providing shelter, education, and vocational training for Chinese girls rescued from sex slavery. A group of dedicated women in charge of running the home formalized their efforts by establishing the **Women's Missionary Society of the Pacific Coast**. The *Oriental* **Home and School** was demolished by the cataclysmic 1906 San Francisco earthquake but was rebuilt at 940 Washington Street, their existing 100–year–old building originally designed by famed architect, Julia Morgan. In the 1940s, the *Oriental* **Home** was renamed as **Gum Moon**—or *Golden Door*!

§

I'd already passed through **Gum Moon**'s solid arched golden door—of mahogany or maple, more like—atop the short flight of nine brick steps, rising up to the front entry to the stately, four–story brick edifice. And I was already inside, standing in front of a tall, sectioned window trimmed in marine green that looked out on Washington Street, pleading my case to the matronly, world–weary–looking residence director with dark, short–styled hair named *Tiffany Tan*.

FRANCESCO FERRARI
EXPLORES CHINATOWN

"I'm sorry, Mister Ferrari," Tan apologized again, adamant. "I'm duty bound to abide by certain professional ethics. And I simply cannot betray the trust, or otherwise compromise the privacy or security of any resident of this shelter—whether past, present, or future. So I can neither confirm nor deny whether the girl you're looking for is even here—in residence."

"Not even if she's in danger?" I persisted. "Believe me, Ms. Tan, if the hoodlums who are after her find out she's here first, they won't ask you so nicely—or politely."

"Not trying to be contrary, Mister Ferrari, but I have only your word for it that this girl could be in any danger from anyone."

"Don't take just my word for it then! Call **SFPD** and contact Inspector Dave Toski in homicide! He'll vouch for me!"

"I couldn't divulge a resident's whereabouts to the police any more than I can divulge it to you, Mister Ferrari!"

"Lookit," I told her agitatedly, "we're really coming down to the wire on this thing and time's running out—fast!"

"I can't accommodate you, Mister Ferrari, I'm sorry."

Just then, another voice—a shrill, feminine outcry—suddenly intruded on our dispute.

"Protect me!" cried the young Chinese girl wandering slowly into the middle of the room. "Soldiers! Soldiers!"

I spun around, taken aback.

"Choy?" I asked. "Are you *Choy Cum*?"

"Protect me!" she pleaded again, a terrified look in her eyes as she pointed frantically toward the front windows. "Protect me!"

I glanced around, sliding to one side of the nearest window, peering outside. I promptly spotted that familiar duo of Chinese toughs, clad in black *changshans*, milling around on the sidewalk below at the foot of the front stairs.

"Time's up!" I told Tiffany Tan urgently. "Those hoods are here! We need to go right now! Is there a back way out of here?"

"There's the side gate down the hill!" Tan declared, conspicuously provoked. "Choy can show you the way!"

"Keep that front door secure!" I bid her in parting. "Call the cops and report a couple of trespassers!"

"Let's go!" I snapped at *Choy Cum*, tugging her along by her tiny waist! "Lead on!"

§

Peering discreetly around the edge of the tall, brick column buttressing the black–grilled gate on either side, I watched intently as that pair of Chinese toughs climbed up those black–railed steps until they were lost to sight inside the front entryway.

"Go!" I bid Choy excitedly, ushering her forward with my arm.

She took off, scuttling downhill toward Stockton Street—taking me in tow—until we came to the corner of the two–story, cream–colored, **Chinese United Methodist Church**, where she felt comfortable enough to pause and catch her breath—before a spangled, golden *cross* engraved in the front facade of the building!

"I want to show you something!" she blurted out, panting slightly.

"Show me something?" I asked, aghast. "Show me what? We've got to get you out of here and protected—as you asked!"

"This is very important!" she insisted. "You must come with me to see!"

Resignedly, I gestured for *Choy Cum* to lead on. Together, we hustled along the busy, two–way thoroughfare,

134

heading northward toward Jackson, the one–way cross street. At Jackson, we bent our hurried steps westward, against traffic—into familiar territory I'd already traversed just recently. Before long, we passed by the **Chinese Hospital** to the left.

Then we ducked into the narrow alleyway adjoining the hospital called **Stone Street**, stepping up to a low–lying doorway on the facing side where—startlingly—*Choy Cum* produced a key to unlock the door, budging it open to let us in!

§

There's been long rumored to exist a fabled *underground* Chinatown—with fanciful and fantastic tales about how the Chinese burrowed down five, six, seven, even *eight* stories underground! It took a cataclysmic earthquake and fire to shatter this long–standing myth and halt this subterranean section's downward plunge into those infernal, nether regions! Chinatown stood up valiantly built upon solid ground, compounded by sound mortar of bygone days.

That engulfing fire which swept through the quarter twenty–four hours after the earthquake was the profoundest disillusioning force. All that it laid bare of those fabulous eight underground levels—after laying the district in ashes—were *basements* as prosaically shallow, and depthless, as any conventional basements found in the city's white sections. Yet the fictitious tale still persists.

Exposed to view, instead, was an inventive labyrinth cleverly constructed out of *connecting* basements and narrow passageways only one level beneath the street! Descending stairways into cloistered cellars created the unreal illusion of plummeting four or five floors into secret spaces of the bowels of the earth! Plumbed were not the depths—but instead a footpath that followed the steep slope or grade of a hill through existing, tilted basements!

Underground Chinatown was no less ominous or sinister because of its shallowness. Its underground chambers were reputedly the setting for unspeakable sins. It harbored filth, disease, murder, and mayhem. It gave safe refuge to habitual gamblers, opium addicts, lepers, tong assassins, and stolen slave–girls. Dead bodies were dumped into its depths. Fat gray rats, foul with vermin carrying bubonic plague germs, scampered freely there.

Down one flight of steps, up another, around a corner, through dark, dank, narrow, and poorly lit passageways—and so it went in those times past.

§

Now I climbed downstairs one flight beneath the street with *Choy Cum*.

"Where are we going, Choy?" I challenged her.

"To see girls trapped like me," she answered in a whispering voice, pausing at the foot of the stairs. "You say you can call the police to help?"

"Yes. Do we need to call them?"

"Right away. Tell them to come to the corner of Washington and Stone Streets to rescue trapped girls like me—right away."

"You mean they're down here in these basements?"

"Yes—through this passage at the end of Stone Street."

"Which side of the street?"

"This side—at the end of this passage."

"Is there anybody chaperoning the girls?"

"Only one guard—a young gang member."

"Hold on!"

I promptly plucked out my mobile phone and speed-dialed Unsavory Dave Toski, **San Francisco Police Department(SFPD)**Inspector 73, my dubious friend and sometime comrade–in–arms:

"Dave!" I accosted him. "Are you busy? Always? Well, get *un*–busy! I need you to come immediately to the corner of Washington and Stone Streets—on the *even* side—preferably with a friend or two—armed and ready to rumble! Yes, in Chinatown! Yes, right now! Is it urgent? Of course, it's frigging urgent! There could be several young ladies' lives at stake! Just get your unsavory butt over here posthaste! I'll meet you there after about a block–long walk! So don't dawdle! It could be a very serious situation! And Dave—don't forget to bring your big gun!"

Then I turned to *Choy Cum*, smiling warmly, gesturing for her to press ahead.

"Why do you do it?" she asked me abruptly.

"Do what, Choy?"

"What puts it into your head to do all this for me when you never saw me before?"

"Let's just say that I enjoy *slumming*!" I joked with a slight chuckle.

She shook her head, befuddled, before starting to shuffle on; and I followed on her heels, pocketing my phone.

As expected, the narrow, winding passageway was dark, dank—and dimly lit by naked, luminous light bulbs set along the way at spaced intervals—as it turned and twisted its way through several small cement cellars, stinking from musty and moldy walls. Strangely, though, we tread a path upwards as we trudged along a gradually uphill incline!

"Dave," I spoke softly into my mobile phone, "please tell me you're outside."

"We're here waiting on you," Toski confirmed. "My partner and I have the corner cordoned off."

"Right."

We plodded ahead, the cragged cement crunching underfoot, until the passageway finally opened out into the last basement—which was far from being empty or vacant.

Several tender young Chinese girls, clothed in traditional loose blue cotton blouses and trousers, were sitting or sprawled around the ramshackle room on small bunks or straw mats. Spread on little folding tables were the discarded dishes of covered pewter, brimming with the remnants of grilled duck, hot soup, noodles, and rice. A tray bearing a tiny bowl with horse chestnuts painted on it was filled with chicken hash, bamboo sprouts and a couple of chopsticks—their festal dish.

Then there was the very youthful Chinese tough—bored, snarling, and mean–looking—slouched against a weathered wall and noticeably nursing a black **QSZ92**, a recoil–operated, locked–breech, semi–automatic pistol, designed by *Norinco*, and holding fifteen rounds of 9X19mm *Parabellum* ammunition. He leapt to his feet, leveling his handgun at me, as soon as he heard my footfalls as I stepped inside the room—keeping *Choy Cum* well behind me.

"What the fuck are you doing here," he spouted crassly, "you *quai lo* asshole!"

"Mind your mouth, son," I told him sedately. "What are you—all of sixteen? Where's your baby–sitter?"

"I can blow you away you *quai lo* motherfucker!"

"Yeah, well, before you do anything stupid with that gun—I strongly suggest that you take a quick peek outside first."

Cautiously, he moved back, keeping his gun pointed toward me, glancing around as he looked out the small, grated, street–level window. And before long, I was budging the low–lying door that opened out to the sidewalk.

Once I ducked through the spare doorway, standing erect to shield my eyes from the shining sun, I frowned—squinting, my brow deeply furrowed, to make out the welcome sight of two unmarked police cruiser cars idled catty–corned to the three–story, cream–colored building.

Next, I sighted old–school, Unsavory Dave Toski, his craggy cheek creased by his ironical grin—both of his arms stiffly outstretched—as he lay prone across the hood of his car, aiming his *Smith & Wesson Model 29*, six–shot, double–action revolver—chambered for the *.44 Magnum* cartridge—straight at me!

TWELVE: A VIRTUOUS PLUM BLOSSOM

"When everything has faded they alone shine forth,
encroaching on the charms of smaller gardens.
Their scattered shadows fall lightly on clear water,
their subtle scent pervades the moonlit dusk.
Snowbirds look again before they land,
butterflies would faint if they but knew.
Thankfully I can flirt in whispered verse,
I don't need a sounding board or winecup."
—Lin Bu, Little Blossom of Hill Garden

Police patrolmen loaded the juvenile Chinese tough, head–down, into the back cage of their police squad car as paramedics loaded those confined young Chinese girls into several of those box–like emergency ambulance vehicles, warning lights swirling, for transport to the **Chinese Hospital** for observation and treatment.

"What in hell have you got yourself mixed up with this time, Frank?" asked Dave Toski pointedly, stepping up to me.

"Something obliquely related to sex trafficking, I think" I told him, "or more specifically, sex *slavery*, as has been pointed out to me."

"Well," he said with his characteristic nonchalance, "it looks like you've dug up a temporary holding pen for a small shipment of trafficked girls. It couldn't have been more perfectly placed, too, as the quartet of gents residing in the apartments upstairs are all elderly Chinese seniors in their eighties!"

"What about the young punk baby–sitting them?"

"You're very lucky he didn't blast you, Mister Ferrari," volunteered the handsome young Chinese plainclothes police officer who came up to us. "He was armed with a pistol used by the Chinese *military*! These gang members are young but they're over–eager and totally foolhardy— and trigger–happy!"

"Meet *Churchill Chiu*," Toski introduced us as we firmly shook hands, "he's on loan to me in homicide from gang task force investigations."

"I'd keep my head down if I were you," I cautioned Chiu good–naturedly, "it's a precarious proposition being Dave Toski's partner!"

"So I've heard," Chiu remarked.

"Churchill's one of our more educated officers," Toski declared. "He graduated from UC Berkeley as he's so fond of reminding us. And he was born and raised in China-town. So he can give you a good primer on the quarter's real inner workings if you need it."

"I do need it," I readily admitted, *"badly!"*

"And I need you to come down to the Central Station on Vallejo Street to make your statement as soon as possible."

"I'll do that," I pledged, "but first—if it's all the same to you—I'd like to talk to *Choy Cum* at the hospital before she's put too deep into protective custody. She's the only one who can really help me on this case I'm working on."

"That's fine," Toski concurred. "As a matter of fact, she's been asking for you, so she trusts you, apparently. Any information you could gather from her about these traffickers would be useful."

"By the way," Toski confided quietly, drawing nearer, "I think I've got a line on those two hoods who attacked you. Ironically enough, they're probably the *Gun* brothers—*Li* and *Leong Yuen Gun.*"

"Scary."

"I can show you their mug shots. One or the other is likely the one who used your gun to kill that girl, *Kum Quai.*"

"Who's no prostitute," I reminded him.

"That remains to be seen. That's what this is really all about, isn't it, Frank?"

"It's my favor to an angel to prove it," I said poignantly.

"Take my advice, Frank," Toski warned me, "don't dig too deep into Chinatown. It truly is a tangled *laby-rinth*—of the best and worst kind. It's a mind–boggling, convoluted *maze* which you could get *permanently* lost in—if you're not very careful."

"Let me talk to *Choy Cum*," I told Toski, ignoring his melodramatic admonition, "right now if you please."

FRANCESCO FERRARI
EXPLORES CHINATOWN

§

Chinese Hospital
845 Jackson Street
Chinatown

Choy Cum sat comfortably in her inclined, white–sheeted hospital bed, propped up by a downy white pillow. She rested her folded hands atop the movable, manila bed–tray positioned across her lap.

Pretty Chinese *plum blossoms*—the oval–shaped petals of the *meihua* with their pointed tips of pink, red, and white—were painted artfully on the wall above her bed's headboard. A vase of purple flowers stood atop the nearby nightstand. And a slender, shaded wall–lamp shed but a shadowed light on the gray–painted room with the hardwood flooring. I sat nearby, relaxed, in a tan vinyl armchair as we talked together.

"There's nothing to ever indicate that you're nearing your life's greatest turning point," *Choy Cum* asked me thoughtfully, "is there, Mister Ferrari? That's the way the biggest things come to us. They don't give any advance notice. They just arrive. And later on, we look back and see how big they really were."

"I suppose so," I ventured, not hazarding any conjecture on my part. "What did you have on your mind?"

"Go back over your own life," she bid me. "Whatever you are today—rich man, poor man, beggar man, thief—wasn't there one man or woman who played a big part in making you what you are? If you're good, wasn't it some one person who made you feel good? If you're bad, wasn't it some one person who was the turning point?"

"I can't say that I've ever thought about it in quite those terms," I admitted, my eyebrows raised by the surprise of her proposition, "but there's good and bad—more

145

or less—in everybody. So why brand yourself as one or the other when life's not that black–or–white?"

"I believe that your whole life," she clarified, "right from start to finish, is just a proposition of one man many times over. First, you meet the one person, then you meet another. And each person stands for some special thing— and stamps you with that thing. Sometimes they don't stamp you very hard, so it doesn't stick. But sometimes, once or twice in your life, a person comes along who's right in line with everything else that's working on you at the time. When that happens, it's a turning point."

"It sounds to me like you're expressing a complicated explanation of *fate*!"

"Really," she said, emphatic, "when you think about it, how much did you yourself have to do with shaping your own life? Mighty little. It was shaped for you. You aren't to be praised for it. You aren't to be blamed. It's almost a joke to speak of it as your life. It's everybody's life."

"Who exactly is this *everybody* you're talking about?"

"I'm talking about the one man who put me where I am!" she blurted out, her eyes welling out. "The one man— for good or bad! He came at just the right moment—or the wrong one!"

"Our lives are full of influential people who affect our fate."

"I'm talking about *Kai Ming*!" Choy Cum cried out at last. "He's the one who brought me to this hateful, dirty life! He's left his stamp on me!"

"Kai Ming?"

"I've been his mistress as well as his whore! And once a whore, always a whore!"

"There's no such thing as a person who can't be degraded," I heartened her. "And there isn't any person who can't be raised. You can change."

"I can't go back now," she said despairingly. "It's not

possible. People don't take backward steps. I've got to go on."

"You've already moved forward by walking through that door."

"I'd always felt the door of escape from this life had been opened—that it stood at least ajar. But where I'd thought to see a way out, it just led into another prison."

"You're not going to prison," I reassured her. "Kai Ming is—if anybody."

"I used to have a love of beauty," she lamented mournfully. "It isn't fair to turn that love of beauty to a girl's ruin. It isn't right. There ought to be some way out of it."

"You've already taken the first step by being here."

"I'm only here because I was afraid for my life," she confessed, shaking her head guiltily, "so I ran away."

"How do you mean?"

"I gave *Kum Quai* my coat to wear the night she was killed. And once I realized it was me that they meant to kill—I ran."

"You can't blame yourself for them killing *Kum Quai*. But why would they have wanted to kill you?"

"Because," she answered, slowly pulling out from her hip an oblong, palm–sized, and rubberized black object maybe one ounce in weight, "they found out that I got away with taking this!"

She handed it over to me, pressing it into my upturned palm, which I laid open: a removable, encased **USB flash drive**, or data storage device with flash memory!

"What's on this?" I asked, awestruck.

"Everything."

"You realize, of course," I told her forebodingly, "you've already risked your life by identifying your manipulators to police. You know enough about their operation to expose it as a criminal enterprise."

"A prostitute is someone who sells herself for money,

Mister Ferrari," she brooded, her voice tinged with profound remorse. "Well, I've wondered, was there anybody according to that who didn't sell themselves for money? Didn't everybody supply some demand—in some more or less disagreeable way? And wasn't everything always for money? So I came to the conclusion that everybody who does something that goes against their best self—just for money—is a prostitute. And I didn't want to be that anymore."

"Sometimes the strongest things in the world are ideas," I emboldened her. "And these are good ideas."

"There's not a soul to help me in my fight, Mister Ferrari," she said in her desperation. "Nobody to give me a hand when I need it. I feel like I'm standing in a bottomless pit, and I have a rope—my guilt. But there's nobody to pull on the other end of the rope."

"Your rope's made of bravery—not guilt," I told her confidently. "And I promise you, I'm going to be the one on the other end pulling it. Trust me."

"Take your cue from those plum blossoms," I added, gesturing to the wall–painting overhead. "Those symbolize resilience and perseverance in the face of adversity."

As Rachel would tell me later on, the plum blossom was also designated as the *National Flower of the Republic of China on Taiwan.*

"When you speak to me, you always say something good—something that means something," she mused. "I'll always remember you as a kindly man with soft brown eyes. You're one of the few men I've ever met who was good to me just for the sake of being good."

"I'm not as kindly as all that," I said with a shake of my head, blushing with embarrassment. "We're all responsible for each other in lots of ways. I was once a Franciscan seminarian. And I've always remembered a certain snippet of what St. Francis once wrote: *Holy charity con-*

founds all evil and carnal temptations—and all carnal fears."

"Sometimes," *Choy Cum* pondered, "I look back to that day when I first entered the life and wish—just as I wished in the early hours of that next morning—that the sun had somehow forgot to rise. But the sun did rise. The sun doesn't care for such things as lost girls. It rises anyway—just to show up our shame all the redder in the light of day. You're never at ease until the sun is out of sight and everything is in the dark again. So I thank you, Mister Ferrari."

"For what, my dear Choy?"

"For helping to make me just a little less afraid of the daylight."

THIRTEEN: STAIRWAY TO HEAVEN

"Is not the way of heaven like the stretching of a bow?
The high it presses down,
The low it lifts up;
The excessive it takes from,
The deficient it gives to.
It is the way of heaven to take from what has in excess in order to make good what is deficient. The way of man is otherwise. It takes from those who are in want in order to offer this to those who already have more than enough.
Who is there that can take what he himself has in excess and offer this to the empire? Only he who has the way.
Therefore the sage benefits them yet exacts no gratitude.
Accomplishes his task yet lays claim to no merit.
Is this not because he does not wish to be considered a better man than others?"
—Lao Tzu, Tao Te Ching, Book Two, LXXVII

FRANCESCO FERRARI
EXPLORES CHINATOWN

VALLEJO STREET STEPS
SAN FRANCISCO, CALIFORNIA

There are plenty of stairways to heaven in this city, so to say, but those commanding views of San Francisco's unique cityscape—its distinctive and uncommon skyline—are the most incomparable.

Perched at the brink of **Telegraph Hill** on Vallejo Street between Montgomery and Sansome Streets, the **Vallejo Street Stairway** is only one block long, but it's heart–stoppingly steep! Comprised of three separate stairways, running roughly parallel to each other, the central stairway is the widest and winds its way through the gardens of surrounding, shingled homes. Two smaller stairways, considerably narrower and steeper than the central stairs, run along the fringes of the gardens straight up the hill. Three separate terraces look out on the **Bay Bridge** and **Treasure Island**.

Those concrete steps connect the **North Beach** neighborhood to **Russian Hill**—the upwardly mobile homes becoming more heavenly with the abrupt ascent. At the foot of the stairway rises a plaster apartment building. Halfway up is perched a shingle–style mansion with a wrought–iron gate. At the top hovers a penthouse deck. They climb up both brims of a rising median of live oaks and shrubs.

Counting landings, it takes one hundred–fifty steps to reach the first terrace of benches, where the towering **Transamerica Pyramid** is to be seen shooting up sky–high in the distance. Another 56 zig–zagging steps take you to Taylor Street, in sight of craggy **Alcatraz** island bulging from the bay. Stone balusters mark the staircase across the street ridge. It takes a hundred–eighteen more steps to attain the hilltop—at the balustrade at the east end of the

153

paved part of the 1000 block of Vallejo Street—where the westward perspective exposes the **Presidio** to view.

Originally a *goat path* between Taylor Street and the Summit, it was converted to a stairway under the direction of *Horatio Livermore. Willis Polk* designed those steps as part of the Vallejo Street improvements at Jones Street. Fourteen elegant street lamps stand at spaced intervals along the Vallejo Street crest and down the stairs.

"I like to come up here to get out of Chinatown," SFPD investigator, Churchill Chiu, confided as we sat down on one of those ubiquitous wooden green benches scattered all over San Francisco, "and to get away from Central Station."

"I can understand that," I sympathized. "It's a peaceful respite."

"Dave Toski tells me you want to be put wise to the real inner workings of Chinatown," he offered.

"More or less."

"It's much the same as the rest of this cliquish and cronyistic town, Mister Ferrari," he readily told me. "Chinatown's run by a traditional and wealthy elite that cares little or nothing about the community's working poor. They maintain and regulate that *underground economy* Malcolm Yang told you about, which permits employers to overwork and underpay immigrant workers. They get away with exploiting working people because they operate outside of the white political system—and its passive and unspoken policy of non-intervention—which enables them to ignore minimum labor standards without worrying about government enforcement. It's a *casual* structure with its own set of rules—and a momentum all its own."

"Casual? How in hell did such a setup like that ever get started?"

"There was a time when many apartments in Chinatown had wall-to-wall beds—each one occupied by three

Chinese in successive eight–hour shifts! Such apartments converted to club rooms that provided temporary accommodations for new arrivals and the unemployed. Through games of *mah–jongg* or poker, immigrants made contacts to get jobs or find partners for joint ventures—or borrow funds or pool resources for starting new businesses. The members of such a circle evolved into a collective called a *Fong*—literally a *Room*. As many as fifty to a hundred of these members came from the same village, shared the same surname, or worked in the same trade."

"So this cooperative structure was imported along with the immigrants?"

"From rural regions in China during the *Ch'ing* dynasty. Under American conditions, though, it's been dramatically transformed."

"How?"

"Immigrants from contiguous villages, who spoke similar sub–dialects of Cantonese, collaborated to form even larger groupings called *huiguans*, which were much more commercially oriented—even though, ostensibly, they continued to carry out charity and mutual–aid functions. They arbitrated disputes among members and secured their obligations in business transactions."

"They acted as creditors and collection agencies, you mean."

"For their more affluent members, yes."

"Who were these more *affluent* members?"

"The *big shots*!" Chiu clarified, "Or the *kiu ling* in Cantonese—or the *chiao lin* in Mandarin."

"*Big shots*?" I chuckled knowingly. "Now it's starting to sound *very* San Francisco!"

"*Big shots* own the shops and restaurants and, as such, become patrons," Churchill explained, nodding his agreement. "They command respect because the other members, as clients, depend on them for favors like jobs, mediation, and protection."

"So I suppose these *big shots* banded together to form profitable partnerships."

"Ultimately," Churchill affirmed, "they set up powerful associations, operating with few established rules, that didn't follow American legal practices. Because they weren't held accountable for money collected from members, officers from powerful clans could buy or sell property for the associations—and pocket the profits. A hierarchy based on wealth evolved within these associations, which became the means by which Chinatown's merchant class maintained dominance and control."

"Over what?"

"Trade monopolies, territories, and similar spheres of influence in certain sections. Because Chinatown is small and the in–fighting intense, most conflicts center on competition for territory."

"*Turf wars* in Chinatown!"

"Building ownership is the ultimate symbol of power in Chinatown," Churchill told me. "Every association locates its headquarters in the territory it claims. Eventually, it'll try to buy up even adjacent buildings. These buildings are located in the core of Chinatown and are worth a great deal of money at today's real–estate values. They generate tens of thousands of dollars in rental income each year. Businesses within that territory are operated only by members of the association—or by entrepreneurs ready to accept its dominance. The rules of the game in Chinatown make the associations the district's basic legitimate entities."

"So Chinatown isn't the big happy family it's puffed up to be?"

"Hardly. By their very nature, associations are clannish and exclusionary. Inevitably, then, that leads to conflicts—sectarian–style conflicts—with other associations.

That's why Chinatown has always been an extremely divided community—despite the impression of outsiders to the contrary."

"So these associations call the shots in Chinatown?"

"It's structured so that the larger traditional associations control Chinatown's governing process. And because of the unspoken policy of non–intervention by white government officials, this casual structure maintains *order in the quarter*—like law. It keeps power concentrated in the hands of the wealthy landlords, merchants, and factory owners."

"These *big shots* sound expert at defrauding their own community."

"They've been known to line their pockets with fees collected from residents. They've also used their positions to promote their private interests."

"It's the same old story, isn't it?" I remarked, shaking my head. "Where do the *tongs* fit in with this setup?"

"Ah," Churchill reacted with a knowing snicker, "few Americans comprehend the tongs. Even the Chinese don't understand them all that well. Some claim the tongs are mutual–aid societies, some say they're secret patriotic fraternities—others say they're nothing but criminal organizations."

"What do you say?"

"Tongs can be all of the above. That's what makes them so confounding."

"Can you *un*–confound them for me?"

"The word tong simply means *chamber*," Churchill expounded. "The tong was patterned after secret, patriotic societies called *Triads*—or *San Ho Hui*—which formed in China hundreds of years ago to overthrow the foreign rule of the Manchus—the Ch'ing dynasty—and restore the Ming dynasty. Triads were so called because their members venerated a trinity composed of Heaven, Earth, and

Man. In the course of centuries, Triads spread worldwide to Chinese communities, particularly in Hong Kong and Southeast Asia. They were introduced to America during the nineteenth century. Tongs, on the other hand, got started in America by members of clans tired of being pushed around by the powerful and prestigious associations.

"Since tong members were unrelated, they pledged allegiance to one another as *brothers in blood oath.* They strengthened their bonds through a secret language, signs, and mystical, religious rituals. Their feud–and–vendetta code pledged them to revenge any wrongs commited against fellow members by outsiders. Violence became necessary for self–defense, so highly organized, professional soldiers—called **Brave Tigers**—comprised their core. Major associations started to hire the tongs to violently resolve conflicts or defend their collective interests."

"Such as?"

"Expanding their territory or maintaining their monopolies, mostly."

"So, the associations were fighting their battles by proxy!"

"The inability of the associations to resolve their conflicts peacefully resulted in the so–called tong wars, which reflected the deep–seated conflicts throughout Chinatown. It was internecine warfare in an ethnic ghetto."

"Wasn't there a criminal side to the tongs?"

"There was the gambling, the opium smuggling, and prostitution—but if the tongs didn't operate these illicit enterprises directly, then they'd extort protection payments from those who did. Wherever they expanded their territory, they extended their protection rackets, too."

"So the community's standards for solving problems was reduced to the lowest common denominator—might makes right."

"And as violence stimulated more violence, the atmosphere of the entire community was poisoned."

"Then there do exist modern–day tongs?"

"Tongs have *always* been a force in Chinatown," Churchill confirmed. "And they've been feared, but the casual political structure in Chinatown has given them official sanction. They've become part of the Establishment—though nobody will acknowledge that fact at public assemblies!"

"Tongs are still Chinatown's dirty little secret then."

"The so–called downtown and uptown Chinese Malcolm Yang told you about rarely come into contact with one another except, possibly, in Chinatown restaurants," Churchill elucidated further. "Check out the wall behind the cash register in most any restaurant or store in Chinatown. You'll see prominently displayed there a framed, printed certificate in Chinese stating that such–and–such tong appreciates the business' generous contribution to its charity fund drive—serving notice that the extorted protection money has been paid."

"So I suspect that these tongs intimidate and terrorize workers just enough to prevent them from reporting or organizing against unfair labor practices."

"Right," Churchill bristled. "That's why I can't stand these pampered, self–appointed, self–indulgent, armchair champions of the oppressed and downtrodden Chinese masses—*Vanessa Hua* over at the *Chronicle* being one of the worst offenders! That spoilt little brat hasn't a fucking clue about what exploitation in Chinatown's all about. I'd really like to see her wash dishes seventy hours for just one week for some tyrant restaurant owner—she wouldn't last one day!"

"What about your local politicians?" I suggested. "They're no help?"

"That's a laugh!" Churchill jeered. "Because of low

voter turnout in Chinese communities, most politicians ignore Chinatown during elections. At best, they'll pay a quick visit during the campaign—to have the television cameras filming them shaking hands with some Chinatown bigwig, or gobbling down an egg roll in front of a Chinese crowd. Otherwise, they don't over–exert themselves campaigning for the Chinese vote. As a result, they owe nothing to the Chinese."

"Do you know Chinatown's supervisor—*Aaron Munchkin?*" Churchill asked me in turn.

"Not personally," I hissed. "I know *of* the runty, little bastard! Once I submitted to him a report recounting my run–in at **Coit Tower** with an Egyptian assassin! He couldn't be bothered to have the decency—or the common courtesy—of giving me even a simple reply, much less an expression of, God forbid, gratitude!"

"That figures," Churchill Chiu asserted at the last. "The bottom line about the essential reality in Chinatown, Mister Ferrari, is that a certain class structure has been forced upon Chinatown—imposed on the community by this powerful and wealthy elite—a casual and callous structure that violates with impunity even the most customary standards of fairness and fair treatment!"

FOURTEEN: *PRECIOUS CARGO*

"When the people lack a proper sense of awe, then some awful visitation will descend upon them.

Do not constrict their living space; do not press down on their means of livelihood. It is because you do not press down on them that they will not weary of the burden.

Hence the sage knows himself but does not display himself, loves himself but does not exalt himself.

Therefore he discards the one and takes the other."

—Lao Tzu, Tao Te Ching, Book Two, LXXII

FRANCESCO FERRARI
EXPLORES CHINATOWN

RACHEL'S IN–LAW
ROSS ALLEY
CHINATOWN

Like *Edgar Allan Poe*'s **Raven**, I mused to myself, amusedly, I went gently rapping and tap-
ping at Rachel's chamber door! Only, once the
door opened up, and the door's shadow fell
across the feminine silhouette standing, shakily, in the
faintly–lit doorway, I was shocked and surprised to see
that it wasn't Rachel who was answering her own door!

"My name's *Chin Qui*," the cute young Chinese girl
with the full lips and frizzy black hair told me as she
stepped up into the rayless alleyway light, "but you can
call me Christina. I'm Rachel's friend."

"My name's Ferrari," I said in turn as our mutual
frowns met, "but you can call me Frank—er, *Francesco*."

Chin Qui bowed her head, shaking it stoically.

"What is it?" I pressed her, concerned. "What's
wrong?"

"Rachel's gone," she said worriedly, lifting up her glis-
tening wet eyes to mine again, "she's missing!"

"What do you mean *missing*?" I exclaimed.

"I mean I think Rachel's been *abducted*," she finally
confided, "by a man called *Kai Ming*!"

§

Darling Dragon Massage Parlor
Second–Floor Building
Jackson Street
Chinatown

Outraged, I went straight to the massage parlor in a
flying fury, stalked up those stairs to the second floor and

163

kicked in the front door so hard that its splintered hinges nearly tore loose from the frame!

Inside, the stern–faced Chinese matron stood stoically at her upright reception desk, looking down her nose at me as if she were awaiting my arrival.

"Mister Ming," she announced sedately, holding out a mobile phone for me to snap up from her hand, "for you."

"Ming!" I growled, quivering with rage. "If you do any harm to that girl, you're a *dead* man, I promise you!"

"Relax, Mister Ferrari," Kai Ming condescended to me over the phone, "you're foaming at the mouth for nothing. We don't kill our young charges as a general rule. They're valuable properties and much too precious for that. Besides, we can't deliver damaged goods to our customers."

"You're not delivering anything to anybody, you *sonofabitch*!"

"I never took you for such an uncouth and vulgar man, Mister Ferrari. Simply return the device, which belongs to us, and you can promptly reclaim possession of your little...*ladylove*."

"How do you know I haven't already made a zillion copies of it? How do you know I haven't turned it over to the police?"

"That would be most unfortunate for everyone involved, including yourself and your ladylove. But we're gambling that you're a lot smarter than that."

"We? Who the hell's *we*?"

"Mister Ferrari, you astonish me! Everything that I do is at the command of our *Kai Yee*—our Godfather! Bring us the device!"

"Hell, you can have the damn thing. It's of no earthly use anyway."

"What makes you think that?"

"Because I've seen it," I let on. "I know what's on it. I know where you are. I know what you're up to. And I'd love to meet this *godfather* of yours.''

"Not unless you have a death–wish, Mister Ferrari," *Kai Ming* remarked. "First things first, though: bring us the device—and then we'll see about granting you an audience with the Godfather."

"Lookit," I scoffed scurrilously, "you can forget that nobility title bullshit. I'm not impressed by some over–glorified pimp! I'm just very curious to find out what kind of degenerate would traffic young girls. So I'll bring your frigging device—tonight!"

"Recall what they say about curiosity, Mister Ferrari."

"You can quote clichés all you like, Ming," I cautioned him, "but don't test me. Just don't test me."

§

Churchill Chiu was intently driving across town Unsavory Dave Toski's dark, full–size, five–door, **Dodge Magnum** station wagon with the 6.1L V8 engine with 5–speed automatic transmission. I was his nervous and worried passenger.

"See," Churchill declared with a frustrated shake of his head, "the tongs quietly continue to operate their illicit activities. Everybody inside Chinatown realizes that the tongs are behind the gangs, but nobody dares to point any fingers. Nothing's changed. Tongs involved with protective associations hire youth gangs to serve as enforcers, controlling gambling, drug–dealing, and extortion in the Chinese community."

"But the youth gangs aren't members of the tongs," I surmised.

"Nope. The tongs just sub–contract the dirty work to the gangs, whom they sponsor."

"How do they get away with that?"

"The tong pays a coordinator to recruit and organize a gang. This coordinator—or *dai low*, meaning elder brother—is often an ex–gang member from Hong Kong who can command a faithful following of young toughs. Gang members follow the *dai low*'s orders and have no direct relations with the tong. All communication, including instructions and money, is between the *dai low* and a middle–level tong official—the *contact*."

"*Kai Ming?*"

"Probably. The gangs protect the gambling houses, deal in drugs, extort money from merchants, and collect loans and protection payments from theaters, nightclubs—and *massage parlors*. They're used to intimidate and silence any opposition. They're provided with apartments, money, cars, guns—and lawyers. Force—or the threat of it—is still the most effective method for the Chinatown elite to command compliance."

"That's a tough system to crack."

"Any direct link between the tong and gang can't be proved. And gang members know that nobody will cross them or report them to the police."

"How do people accept that situation?"

"It's understandable," Churchill explained, sympathetic, "that people in Chinatown understate the enigma of the tongs. They live and work in the community and have noplace else to go. When confronted with criminal threats, they have to be practical. That's why so many businesses pay protection money. It's cheaper to pay a few hundred dollars a month than to get their storefront window shattered—or their family's safety threatened."

"That's a helluva thing to have to get used to," I said, sighing heavily.

"Showing fight's made even tougher," Churchill said with a knowing nod, "by these newbie fat–cat investors from the Far East—especially property developers and real–estate speculators spending overseas capital—who monopolize Chinese immigrant labor. That's the real, so—called *gentrification* of Chinatown."

"Or," I speculated, "who exploit young immigrant girls."

Just then, Churchill Chiu warily pulled up the **Dodge Magnum** to *Cargo Way*—off Third Street on the southern waterfront—bound for the deep—water berth of **Pier 96** at the **Port of San Francisco**.

FIFTEEN: PYRAMID POWER

"When peace is made between great enemies,
Some enmity is bound to remain undispelled.
How can this be considered perfect?
Therefore the sage takes the left–hand tally,
but exacts no payment from the people.
The man of virtue takes charge of the tally;
The man of no virtue takes charge of exac-
tion.
It is the way of heaven to show no favourtism.
It is for ever on the side of the good man."
—Lao Tzu, Tao Te Ching, Book Two, LXXIX

FRANCESCO FERRARI
EXPLORES CHINATOWN

Port of San Francisco
Pier 96
Deep—Water Berth

San Francisco's southern waterfront is somewhat isolated and remote—not only out of the
way, but also out—of—sight—and—out—of—mind
compared to the rest of the breezy city. To the
north, colossal, metallic, heavy—lift, *Erector Set*—like cargo
cranes—their monstrous contours silhouetting the night
sky—loomed ahead in the lurid darkness. Beyond, the
sparkling cityscape sprawled across the placid sea line.

Two, towering white lamps irradiated the shoreless
pier, an expansive area spreading over thirty acres of solid
dock space. Moored alongside the pier, resting unbudging
in its deep—water berth, a gigantic Chinese cargo freighter
hovered sky—high over the open space like some enormous
behemoth! Along with Churchill Chiu, buffeted by the
gentle bay breeze, I gradually climbed the ship's rising
gangplank—bound for the gaping gangway in the ship's
bulwark. Atop the sloping gangplank, we were confronted
by Kai Ming together with his two snarling henchmen,
Hunter and Murray.

"Good evening, Mister Ferrari," Kai Ming addressed
me snidely. "You were told to come alone. Who's this *hea-
then Chinee* with you?"

"This is *my* bodyguard," I proudly announced. "Allow
me to introduce, Mister Chiu!'"

Before anybody could reply or react, Churchill whipped
out his *Glock 20*—that *.40 S&W* version of the full—sized,
polymer—framed, short recoil—operated, locked—breech,
semi—automatic *Glock 17* pistol favored by law enforcement—and thrust its barrel firmly into Kai Ming's throat,
tugging him aside roughly by his coat lapel.

"Your pieces," I demanded, stepping straight up to

Hunter and Murray, "thumb–and–forefingers if you please."

Snarling in defiance, the pair hesitated.

"You're under arrest for human smuggling and sex trafficking," Churchill informed Kai Ming with another emphatic prod of his gun barrel. "And so is this vessel—*in rem!*"

"*Against all the world*, eh?" Kai Ming remarked. "How do you expect to enforce that arrest—alone?"

On time, a squad of police cruiser cars—sirens blaring, blue lights swirling—screeched onto the pier's Tarmac, speeding up to the ship in force!

"The *SWAT* team's on board, too," Churchill added sedately.

"Do it," Kai Ming ordered the two toughs. "Hand over your guns."

"Go fetch Miss Chung," I told the two as I pulled the magazines from their pistols before tossing them aside, pocketing the magazines, "and escort her here nicely—like gentlemen. *Now!*"

Just then, the first detachment of armed police officers started tramping up the gangplank's lengthy incline.

"Mister Ming here is a *snakehead*," Churchill related as he started frisking him for weapons.

"That's not the term I'd use," I cracked.

"I'm not armed," Kai Ming grumbled.

"He specializes in smuggling scores of girls in the hidden cargo holds of major freighters that cross the Pacific to ports like San Francisco," he qualified. "Starved, deprived of fresh air and sunlight, beaten regularly—many get shackled and handcuffed to metal bed frames for the duration of the excursion—to break their spirit!"

"Like I told you, Ming," I said, stepping up to him closely, "that flash drive's just a bonus. *Choy Cum* rendered it superfluous. She's safe in protective custody. She's

172

a material witness. And right now, she's spilling to investigators all about your little loveboat cruise."

"Profits above all," Churchill Chiu said scornfully, "no matter what the human cost!"

"Mister Ming," I whispered to him confidentially, "just between you and me—tell me where I can find this almighty *godfather* of yours."

"I'm exceedingly glad to tell you where you can find our Godfather," Kai Ming accommodated me arrogantly, "because I know that when you finally meet him, he will put you away—permanently."

"I was hoping you'd say something like that."

§

"I'm just so happy to be in your sweet, loving arms, Francesco," Rachel told me feelingly once I enfolded her after we were reunited at the pier terminal.

"I'm just glad you're safe and sound," I said, embracing her warmly about the light blanket paramedics had wrapped around her shoulders. "I'm sorry I was late. I was supposed to be the one guarding you this time."

"If I'm an angel," she kidded me, "then I'd like to go back to heaven as soon as possible—or, no, maybe to my Africa first."

"First," I insisted, "you're going back home with Mister Chiu."

"You're not coming with me?"

"No, I can't right now. I've got someplace else to go— another errand to run."

"Do you know what, Francesco?"

"What, dearest?"

"This Bay Area is supposed to be some kind of paradise, right?"

"So they say."

"Well," Rachel said disgustedly, "all I have to say is—this is just another shitty day in paradise! And if this is paradise, hell can't be too bad—so I'd rather go to hell!"

"That doesn't sound like you, my Angel" I told her, folding her in my arms even more snugly. "Besides, there's no place for an angel except heaven. And right now, for you, *home* is where heaven is—and *home* is where you're going!"

"Where are *you* going?"

"To see a *chiao lin*—a big shot!"

§

Transamerica Pyramid
600 Montgomery Street
San Francisco, CA

Towering sky–high between Clay and Washington Streets in the city's Financial District, its rough facade covered in crushed quartz, the four–sided, 48–story **Transamerica Pyramid** shoots up 853 feet—its illuminated, aluminum–paneled cap brightly piercing the heavens. Amongst the asphalt jungle of 27 skyscrapers and 482 high–rises, the pyramid once ranked as the tallest edifice in San Francisco's skyline until that atrocious **Salesforce Tower** surpassed it in 2018.

At midnight, I was being led at gunpoint through the pyramid's four–story, concrete, slab–like base by a gang of young Chinese toughs, our footsteps echoing off the lobby walls, escorted on either side by those *Gun* brothers—*Li* and *Leong Yuen*, who was still nursing the busted nose I'd given him in that alleyway a while back.

"*Leong!*" his name was summoned with a squelching sound.

"Yes, Godfather?" Leong replied, speaking into his

Motorola walkie–talkie, a hand–held, portable, metal–encased, two–way radio transceiver.

"After he's thoroughly searched," ordered the starchy yet throaty Chinese voice on the other end, "bring Mister Ferrari to the conference room on the forty–eighth floor."

"Yes, Godfather!"

"There must be twenty elevators in this building," Leong Yuen said, concerned, "which one do we take?"

"There's eighteen to be exact," Li Gun corrected him, "but only two reach the top floor—which is the conference room—so we'll have to figure out which is which. I only know of the one."

"You know," I started, interrupting them, "if you two hadn't jumped me in that alley that night, I would never have gotten involved in this thing."

"Shut the fuck up, Ferrari!" Li Gun snapped.

"Who hired you to hit me?"

"Nobody."

"*Nobody*? What in hell did I do to deserve your charity then?"

"Nothing."

"*Nothing*?"

"We saw you at the **Li Po** and didn't like the look of you. So we decided to roll the drunk."

"You mean it was a totally *random* gesture of your goodwill?"

"Totally."

"If that's all it was," I said, scrupulous, stopping dead in my tracks, "you should've just said so—I could've told you the feeling was mutual."

Just then, we came up to the shiny bank of golden metal elevator doors, where Li Gun proceeded to carefully frisk me from head to toe after leaning me against a wall.

"This time might be different, Ferrari," Li Gun growled in my ear with a snarl, "if the Godfather tells me to put you away—like I took out that little slut, *Kum Quai!*"

"So *you're* the one—" I muttered to myself in shock.

Once the wall–panel button was pressed and those elevator doors hissed wide open, I made my most impulsively—and explosively—violent move! Without warning, I forcefully stiff–armed Li Gun's solar plexis with a right palm–heel strike, making him cry out in pain as I spun him abruptly around—promptly locking his head in a choking Japanese stranglehold! As I did so, I dragged him backwards—bodily—across the elevator threshold! His handgun clattered to the elevator floor.

"Get back!" I threatened the others, both of my enfolding arms tightly locking his head, one arm in front, the other arm behind. "Or I'll break his fucking neck!"

Grudgingly—unsteadily—the others stood aside.

"Hit the forty–eighth floor!" I growled into Li Gun's ear, throttling him tightly. "I'll break your windpipe!"

Gasping for air, Li Gun strained every nerve to reach out to press the top–floor elevator button!

"Loy gee, hai dai!" I barked, shouting my sole smattering of Chinese that translated roughly to: *Come on, you cowards!*

Those elevator doors hissed tightly shut.

"You're lucky I don't kill your ass!" I roared furiously, hurling him hard against the confined elevator wall as I hammer–fisted his battered face—repeatedly, ragefully—until I knocked him senseless!

As he lolled, sprawled unconscious on the elevator floor, I snapped up his **QSZ–92**—the recoil–operated, locked–breech, semi–automatic pistol. I pulled–and–pushed snug its dual stack magazine, holding fifteen rounds of 19X19 *Parabellum* ammunition. Like many modern military pistols, it had a familiar double–action, single–action trigger with a combined safety–decocker. Then I anxiously awaited the long slog of the ascent as the elevator climbed

176

decidedly upward, slowly scaling the city heights!

Predictably, once those elevator doors hissed open again at the forty–eighth floor—where I deliberately punched the red *emergency stop* button to hang up the idled elevator car—a barrage of bullets pulverized the elevator doorsill, riddling the body propped up there, shattering the rear wall! Mine wasn't the body darkening the door-way though—it was Li Gun's, gripped and held up from one side, behind the elevator front, by the scruff of his murderous neck! Now, he was murdered, wrenched from my grasp, by a fusillade of fire from some deadly assault rifle!

Before that shooter ever knew what hit him, standing so squarely and smugly in the open, I promptly dropped down on one knee, my arms stiffly outstretched as I as-sumed the firing position—taking careful aim to return fire with multiple rounds of Li Gun's pistol! After the shooting stopped, I could make out the hulking figure of the other shooter, sprawled across the room in a rumpled, lumpish heap.

"Come in, Mister Ferrari," I was bid calmly by the guttural Chinese voice, "I am quite alone and unarmed."

"Come out where I can see you first," I demanded.

At the mouth of a railed stairway, situated unexpect-edly in the center of the coffee–carpeted conference room, the tall, gaunt, and imposing, square–jawed Chinaman with the strikingly sharp features, stepped slowly into full view.

"You killed a good man," he lamented, gesturing gen-tly to the dead body behind him, "my bodyguard. I called him Chuck Lee in honor of *Lee Chuck*—the famed body-guard to *Little Pete*, another great godfather."

Leveling my pistol at the Chinaman from my hip, I moved around to the body to make doubly sure it was un-moving.

"Maybe you ought to re–think hiring Occidental bodyguards," I remarked. "They're too trigger–happy in my experience."

"This is, indeed, a very dark hour for business," the Chinaman deplored.

"*Business*? Is that what you call it?"

"Yes—a business with a powerful profit motive sub-ject to the market forces of supply and demand."

"Sick," I said, moving around nearby to the shiny, rectangular conference table surrounded by ten swivel chairs.

"Quite the contrary, Mister Ferrari," the Chinaman maundered, "you can't be that naive."

With my free hand, I snapped up a mobile phone from the tabletop, punching up numbers as I aimed the pistol directly at the Chinaman—for emphasis—to stay still.

"Dave," I reported to Unsavory Dave Toski, homicide Inspector 73 for the **SFPD**, "**Transamerica Pyramid**. For-ty–eighth floor. Conference Room...you're airborne—and you've got my back."

I glanced around the room with its ocher–colored walls lined with rows of tall, rectangular windows, exposing the sparkling city to panoramic view on all sides.

"Watch for my signal from the front face," I added be-fore signing off.

"My men will be ascending those stairs as we speak, Mister Ferrari," the Chinaman boasted. "You're literally living on borrowed time."

"I wouldn't gloat," I admonished him. "If they show up—*your* time's up!"

"Why did you come here? To express your pious, self–righteous indignation?"

"I came to see you close up shop!"

"Mister Ferrari," the Chinaman laughed aloud, "you're a simple–minded fool! You can't simply shut up shop! The sex industry is something akin to a giant, mature, multi–national corporation. It's achieved steady–state growth and produces tremendous cash flows!"

"And I suppose your're the corporate CEO?"

"Indeed," he proudly replied, "I am. My name is *Leong Chong Po*! I come from the *tien–hsia*—the China Empire!"

"You're no CEO," I told him contrarily, "you're just a *kwei chan*—a villain."

"How silly and childish you are, Mister Ferrari," *Leong Chong Po* jeered. "The sex industry generates billions of dollars in profits each year—at a profit margin greater than almost any other industry in the world—illicit or otherwise. It's a high–profit, minimal–risk venture. Sex workers are by far the most lucrative workers in the world. One woman is trafficked for the purpose of sexual pleasure every sixty seconds—dispersed all across the globe! Sex *sells*!"

"Minimal risk? For who? The young girls brutalized?"

"Mister Ferrari," *Leong Chong Po* expounded, "the most effective method for any business to increase profits is to minimize costs. For most businesses, the largest operating cost is labor. And sex workers provide *cheap* labor. Maintaining sex workers requires minimal effort since they can be sold for sex services literally *thousands* of times before being replaced. One young female, you see, can be used by numerous customers over and over—time and time again."

"You scum–sucker!" I spouted disgustedly. "These are human beings—not *recyclables*!"

"Recyclables? Like the subservient wives of husbands, you mean?"

"You're not selling enslavement to me, Mister *Po*!"

"*All* men want women as slaves—even you, Mister Ferrari."

"Don't ever presume to speak for me, Po!"

"Nevertheless," he persisted, "it's the pervasive male demand to purchase sex that provides the perfect environment for the proliferation of the sex industry. There could be no industry without this male demand for commercial sex. That demand has propelled the industry for centuries—and it will probably continue to do so for centuries to come!"

"Speaking of things that propel things—" I pondered as I moved around once more to the Chinaman's dead henchman.

Bending a knee, I promptly snapped up his dropped weapon—a **QBZ–95**, a *Type 95* automatic bullpup assault rifle, capable of firing the small–caliber, high–velocity, 5.8X42mm DBP87 intermediate cartridge at a rate of 650 rounds per minute! Its selector switch was set for 2—or fully automatic!

"It's time for you to take a walk on the wild side, Mister *Po!*" I taunted him, waving him over to a window overlooking the soaring tower's frontward face.

"I don't know what you expect to gain by closing down my organization, Mister Ferrari," he quibbled dubiously, "mine is just a single cog in a mighty machine!"

"You know what they say—one cog at a time. Open it up!" I ordered him.

Ingeniously, **Transamerica Pyramid** windows swiveled on a rotating pivot so that they could be cleaned inside!

Tucking the pistol inside my waistband, I manipulated the assault weapon with both hands—pulling the charging handle fully to the rear, releasing it forward to bring a round into the chamber, readying it to fire!

"Straddle the window–sill!" I ordered him.

"You're mad, Mister Ferrari," he said worriedly.

"Isn't everybody? Straddle it, I said!"

I pointed the weapon's barrel at him emphatically.

"I can't!" he cried, grasping the window frame shakily

as he lifted a leg over the sill by grudgingly slow degrees. A blustering gust of wind wafted up and down his whole body.

"What's the matter, Mister Po?" I derided him angrily. "You're not afraid to take a dive from the forty–eighth floor, are you? Or, are you afraid of being *disposable*—like all those young girls you've enslaved?"

"Mister Ferrari—*please...*"

"Well!" I bellowed at him, yanking him by his neck and shoving until he hung, wobbling, halfway out of the window. "How does it feel to be *disposable*?"

That's when I heard the thunderous rumble of the powerplant of *Turbomeca Arriel* 2C2–CG turboshaft engines belonging to the twin–engined helicopter, manned by a double pilot–and–crew, hovering high up overhead!

Wrenching *Leong Chong Po*, I jerked him back into the room, roughly spun him around, and deftly chopped the nape of his neck with the rigid ridge of my hand—knocking him out!

Hovering into view, the *United States Coast Guard Eurocopter MH–65 Dolphin* rent the air—the rackety whirring of its rotor blades reverberating throughout the night. In response to my frantic waving at the window, the helicopter started lowering its compact, cable–suspended, single–person rescue basket—slowly, swaying in the whistling wind—to the outer facade of the lofty edifice! Once it was within reach, I strapped myself into its harness, shuddering in fear at the terrifying, dizzying sight of the ground plummeting so out of reach—so far off below. Clutching the Chinaman tightly to my chest—the boisterous gusts smiting my face—I gnashed my teeth and squeezed my eyes tightly shut as the rescue basket started its interminably slow crawl upward. For the longest time, we dangled there in midair as we were hoisted sluggishly to safety inside of the helicopter. I'd felt as if I'd been hanging by a thin thread over a volcano!

I'd lost my grip on the assault weapon, letting it clatter to the carpet of the room as the helicopter's rescue basket hauled us up from the open window. Just then, *Leong Yuen Gun*, together with the rest of *Leong Chong Po*'s gang of youthful toughs, had emerged en masse from the mouth of that room's central stairway! Side by side, they scrambled to the swivel windows, preparing to open fire on us with their own guns! But dependable Unsavory Dave Toski thwarted them!

From its tripod mount, his satirical grin creasing his craggy cheek, Toski fired a volley from the helicopter's belt–fed, gas–operated, medium, 1X7.62mm **M240 machine gun**—shattering the crushed quartz facade at the base of the conference room's row of windows!

Finally, I settled next to Toski, breathing a sigh of profound relief as the helicopter perceptibly gained altitude!

"Meet the Chinese godfather!" I bid him with an ironical smile of my own, bellowing above the rackety roar of the helicopter. "He told me he wants to go legit! He told me he's thinking about investing in the *recycling* business!"

SIXTEEN: CHANGING WINDS

*"The way is empty, yet use will not drain it.
Deep, it is like the ancestor of the myriad
creatures.
Blunt the sharpness;
Untangle the knots;
Soften the glare;
Let your wheels move only along old ruts.
Darkly visible, it only seems as if it were there.
I know not whose son it is.
It images the forefather of God."*
—Lao Tzu, Tao Te Ching, Book One, IV

FRANCESCO FERRARI
EXPLORES CHINATOWN

THE BUENA VISTA CAFE
2765 Hyde Street

America's First Irish Coffee Was Made Here
in 1952
—exterior wall plaque

The *Buena Vista*, so reads its iconic sign, ablaze in blood–orange neon, and overhanging the entrance to the hundred–plus–year–old, three–story, laurel green building situated at the corner of Hyde and Beach Streets at the foot of the Powell–Hyde cable car line at the northern bayfront. Close to the street corner, next to a light post, stands a lone, scraggly tree draped in what look like perennially unseasonal Christmas lights. Before opening its first floor as a saloon in 1916 it operated as an old boarding house.

For me, the place is still a boarding house; it's where I call home in the city—though there was a presentiment in the air portending all that was about to change.

Through the battered, weatherbeaten front double doors, a narrow passage is cut through the length of the interior—with the long, polished, mirrored–and–wooden antique bar sidled with tall, wooden barstools on one side; a row of round–topped, wooden tables–with–chairs set at spaced intervals next to tall, arched windows on the other. Overhead globe lights and fans hang from the ceiling. Underfoot, shoe soles scuff across octagon–patterned floor tiles.

As usual, like clockwork, a pair of brotherly, white–jacketed bartenders step up to the bar, lining up straight in a row ten or twelve six–ounce, stemmed, tulip–shaped glasses, and plunking into each a couple white sugar cubes. From a diner–style pot, they pour into the glasses a continuous, steaming stream of hot black Colombian coffee.

In another long, dramatic stream all along the assembly line of standing goblets is poured the Tullamore D.E.W. Irish Whiskey. Finally—with a grand finale gesture, from an upright blender—the frothy collars of heavy but lightly whipped whipping cream are dolloped out easily over a spoon. And so the illustrious legend of the *Buena Vista*'s celebrated Irish coffee is so regularly perpetuated.

§

Thanks to the generosity of the saloon's gracious proprietors—the husband–and–wife team of Nolan Quinn and Beverly London, who lovingly own and run the place—I maintain a modest home office in the smallest, third–floor flat upstairs, overlooking the Powell–Hyde Street cable car turnaround and the adjoining grassy **Victorian Park**. At the back of the first–floor bar a cramped space, enclosing a blue–hued, ebony *Steinway & Sons Pops Collection* grand piano is cordoned off with a red velvet, brass post–supported rope line. Nolan often frequents the bar while his wife, Beverly, regularly plays piano and sings standards and torch songs from the Great American Songbook.

At the far end of the bar at the rear of the room at the lone, little table nearest the piano, Rachel and I sat together, holding hands, slurping our own pair of Irish coffees—playfully comparing the mustaches on our upper lips made from sipping the frothy foam topping the drinks. Space at this boisterous–and–bustling place was always at a premium, but this night, happily, was spare of patrons and exceptionally quiet.

"It's so good seeing you like this again, Francesco," effused Beverly, "I haven't seen you this healthy—and happy—since..."

"I know," I said seriously with a nod of acknowledgment, "but it's all down to my beautiful guardian angel here."

"We're so glad you brought her to introduce us."

"Blessedly," I joked as an aside, "she's not one of these frustrated *Asian*–Americans terminally complaining about the trials and tribulations of assimilation!"

"Don't mind him," Beverly reassured Rachel, "being obnoxious is second nature sometimes."

"I don't mind," Rachel demurred. "Besides, Asian–American is just another artificially contrived generic label—no better or worse than *Oriental*."

"Or person *of color*," I interjected with a grunt, "which is just a *colored* person without the preposition."

"I thought it was supposed to signify ethnic pride," Beverly offered.

"All that's so fake and phony," Rachel told her. "If I want to express pride in my ethnic identity, then I prefer simply being called what I am: *Chinese*! Obsessing over semantics only blinds shallow and superficial people to things that are truly important."

"Fair enough," Beverly beamed. "And those growing pains of assimilation—not too hurtful, I hope."

"Only if you listen to the like of actress, Sandra Oh, telling the rest of us what *victims* we're all supposed to be!" Rachel answered, unflinching. "I'm nobody's *victim*, Beverly. Nobody forces us to come to America—whether immigrants or visitors. We reap what we sow by choosing to come here. How can we complain about the consequences of choices we freely make? Only the self–serving do that."

"That's my girl," I said smugly.

"All those put–on labels were probably invented by some stuffy and pretentious Cantonese—*ng soung*!" Rachel said.

"What?" Beverly and I asked almost in unison.

"*Uptight!*" she translated, making us laugh. "No kidding, they're my beloved brethren, but I think the Cantonese are the most talkative and big–mouthed people in all the world!"

"I hope they speak well of you, too," I joked with a chuckle.

Just then, Nolan Quinn stepped up to the table, grim–faced.

"I hate to crash your party," he started, sounding glum, "but I've got something pretty important to tell you that can't wait."

"Sure, Nolan," I invited him, gesturing to a chair, "sit down and speak your piece!"

"It's the bastard landlord," he confided bitterly. "Our lease is up for renewal next month. They not only intend to jack up the rent to an exorbitant amount—they plan on changing the terms and conditions of the lease by adding a ton of obnoxious clauses. It's really outrageous!"

"Such as?"

"For one thing, they want to dress up all my bartenders in monkey suits and turn the serving of Irish Coffee into an assembly line–style production for the benefit of the tourists! The whole idea is to cater to the tourists over the locals!"

"Turning the place into a *tourist trap!*"

"A circus freak–show, more like."

"You can challenge it, of course."

"That would tie us up in the courts for months—it's hardly worth the effort. Besides, I doubt that we could handle the cost."

"Unbelievable, Nolan, I'm so sorry," I commiserated.

"The worst part is," he added irately, "are their thankless, *ingrate* attitudes. We've given them—and this place—literally *years* of hard labor, devotion, even love. And they're throwing all that patronage right back in our faces like it means nothing, like we mean nothing, treating us like *nobodies—nonentities!*"

"What will you do?" I asked him hesitantly.

"Beverly and I have talked it over," Nolan said with a shrug, "and we're seriously thinking about moving the whole shebang over to some nice spot on Ocean Beach—and cater to a whole new and different crowd—both locals and tourists alike. *Ocean Beach Cafe* over on La Playa's doing very well out there. And we've always adored the outer Richmond hood."

"Sometimes change is good, I suppose," I said dubiously. "Life moves on. All I can say is, wherever you two relocate to—you can count me in!"

"Thanks, Frank," Nolan Quinn told me gratefully, getting to his feet. "I'm sorry for springing this on you just now, but time isn't on our side with this thing."

"It's a great pleasure having you with us, too, Miss Rachel," he added, turning to address her. "Frank is like family. And we're glad having him back in the fold—and having him looking so happy again. You were just what he needed, evidently, and we can't thank you enough for making Frank, well, Frank again! And for bringing him back to us in one piece!"

"Okay," I kidded him with Rachel reacting by poking me in the ribs, "enough with the speech–making. You're starting to sound like you're standing for the Irish Parliament!"

"Again," Nolan apologized again before excusing himself, "pardon the intrusion."

"You have wonderful friends who cherish you as I do, my Francesco," she told me, squeezing my hands caressingly. "Now I have another favor—a final favor—to ask of you."

"Anything, my angel, you know that."

"I would like you to take me home," she said simply,

"and make love to me one last time."

"*Last* time?" I asked, qualmish. "Why should it ever be the last time for us?"

"You will always be the *san doy*, my dear Francesco," she told me.

"The what?"

"The *bachelor*," she translated. "You are like the meal's *dessert*. I'm afraid that your wandering heart could never be sturdy enough to be totally devoted to one woman only—okay then, to one *girl* only—to me only."

"But I've never loved an angel before. And I have no desire to ever stop loving her."

"Then we both have reason to regret," she said sullenly. "There is a Chinese saying—*a person can never tell what life is who has never cried all the night through.* And I think the time has come for us to cry the night through together."

Bewildered beyond belief, I felt hit between the eyes, yet we both sat staring through each other for some moments.

"You two are getting pretty intense over there," Beverly observed, interrupting us. "Let me sing you a song."

"Your discretion, Beverly," I told her absentmindedly, nodding my accord.

Beverly London played for us, **We'll Be Together Again**, a 1945 popular song composed by Carl T. Fischer with lyrics by Frankie Lane. And, as always, she rendered it beautifully for us:

> *"Here in our moment of darkness*
> *Remember the Sun has shone*
> *Laugh and the world will laugh with you*
> *Cry and you cry alone*
> *No tears, no fears*
> *Remember, there's always tomorrow*

FRANCESCO FERRARI
EXPLORES CHINATOWN

So what if we have to part
We'll be together again
Your kiss, your smile
Are memories I'll treasure forever
So try thinking with your heart
We'll be together again
Times when I know you'll be lonesome
Times when I know you'll be sad
Don't let temptation surround you
Don't let the blues make you bad
Some day, some way
We both have a lifetime before us
For parting is not goodbye
We'll be together again."

§

Rachel's In–Law
Ross Alley
Chinatown

Days later, after that last night we'd made love together for that last time, missing her terribly, I couldn't help
but return to Chinatown to try and see her and be with
her. And once more I was met at the door not by Rachel,
but by her good and faithful friend, Christina.

"She's gone again, Francesco," Christina told me stoically.

"What do you mean gone?" I asked irritably. "I'm so
tired of this game!"

"It's no game. She's gone for good this time. I'm sorry."

"Sorry? Is that it? Gone! Sorry!"

"No," she demurred, bowing her head, "she left me a
message to give you should you come looking for her."

"Well, I've come!" I said impatiently. "Where is it—

191

this message?"

"It's not written down," she said solemnly, taking me by surprise. "I'm meant to recite it for you in person."

Supremely perplexed, I waited with bated breath, speechless.

"*My dear Francesco,*" Christina started, articulating her words most meticulously. "*I am not well. In fact, I am very unwell. So much so that I must go to that other world to get well. So I am going back to my home in Taiwan. You must not try to find or follow me.*

"*I feel you have suffered much pain in your life already. I have no wish to hurt you or cause you more.*

"*You call me your angel. You needed the helping hand that I gave you like a sinking man needs a piece of floating wood to cling to. But you no longer need it now. Besides, a broken piece of wood can be of no use to you anymore. And I am broken, my Francesco. From now on, no one else can save your life except yourself.*

"*Should we sing or should we grieve for this forbidding tragedy in our life? For all I have learned in my life, I fail to understand the way of life after all.*

"*All I do know for sure is this: even though I will not be able to be with you, remember—I will always be there in spirit whenever you need me; I will always love you and care for you; I will always stand with you. And I wish the love you feel from me will always warm your heart. All I ask of you in return is that you take care of yourself, as if I were there myself to take care of you.*

"*For beyond all the confusion, beyond all the difficulties of this life—is my undying and unfailing love for you. So let a thousand words turn into one: love.*

"*Your beloved Shih.*"

For the longest time, I was so choked by the rawest emotion, that I was completely numb and powerless to move—or utter even the first word of any sensibility.

EPILOGUE: *TEMPLE TEARS*

"Your name or your person,
Which is dearer?
Your person or your goods,
Which is worth more?
Gain or loss,
Which is the greater bane?
That is why excessive meanness
Is sure to lead to great expense;
Too much store
Is sure to end in immense loss.
Know contentment
And you will suffer no disgrace;
Know when to stop
And you will meet with no danger.
You can then endure."
—Lao Tzu, Tao Te Ching, Book Two, XLIV

FRANCESCO FERRARI
EXPLORES CHINATOWN

Contemporary people in San Francisco look, but they don't *see*. They talk, but they don't *think*. Because they do neither, they rarely *feel*. Real life, though, lies in the essentials, not the trifles.

Hark back to Chinatown of old, and you could find delicacies known as thousand–year ages, imported from China, sitting on merchants' wooden display tables covered in layers of ash, clay, and salt.

Or, you could see stalls, rivaling **Fisherman's Wharf**, which specialized in seafood, such as white–bait–type fish and eight–inch–long squid with their tangle of suction–cupped arms and feelers. Others carried dried foods: shriveled brown oysters skewered on bamboo, dried abalone, dried pig livers, dried squid, and dried seaweed for soups. Some shopkeepers decorated their windows with rows of red–skinned crispy ducks, which they hung by their feet after drying, salting, and pressing them in oil.

In Chinese herb shops, proprietors hung dried gourds above their counters each morning so that customers would know they were available to diagnose constipation, indigestion, and other complaints. To boost male potency, the herbalists might mix up a potion of ginseng, wolfberry, and the aptly labeled *horny goat weed*—sold today as bottled capsules in most health stores.

Candle makers operated out of little holes–in–the–wall. They'd first take a strip of bamboo and wind paper about it. This paper was the wick. Into a big pot of either hot green or vermilion tallow they'd next dip the bamboo. When the proper amount of grease adhered to the stick they'd swing it and roll it into shape, hanging it on a wire line to dry. All about them were bowls of green, red, and yellow paint, and gold leaf on a pink–and–green platter. Their dipping done, they started the task of decoration at which they worked with incredible swiftness.

Festival candles were made of soft tallow, carved into

numberless fantasies: dragons and roses and holy pagodas—red and green with pricking of gold if the occasion
was one of magnificence. Those were for altars and ancestral shrines. And often they burned pallidly at funeral cel-
ebrations.

§

Today, you could still find old–school shops filled with
decorous objects of art bearing the stamp of workman-
ship and taste. You could still chance upon unexpected
treasures in fruit stalls or meat shops: green pink plates
filled with mincing ladies flirting with equally mincing
mandarins; a sandalwood box for trinkets, brown with
age and richly carved; a benign Confucius done in yellow and green porcelain; a copper hand–warmer centuries
old; a fan of guinea–fowl feathers painted with garlands
of bright pink roses; exquisite figurines molded out of rice
paste from which can be built up a complete *Manchu* court
processional.

There's likewise to be seen in the butcher shops whole
pigs strung up by their hindquarters, smoking hot, and
roasted to rich mahogany. These shops boast other fantastic wares: ducks, smoked and flattened to incredible thin-
ness; a curious sausage without casing, rolled into a greasy
mass about a bit of bamboo stick; soyabean cakes; stalks
of wild mustard with the yellow bloom still on them; and
sprouting horse–beans. Often, in a moist tub at the curb,
sit sea–snails and ancient eggs incased in mud.

Exquisite chemist shops of another civilization remain the rule. These chemist shops are the quarter's true
beauty spots. Their walls and doorways are heavy with
black and gilded carvings, and back of their counters rise
tier upon tier of drawers splashed with lacquered paint.
In these rest the herbs forming the basis of Chinese cura-
tives. During slack hours the clerks could be seen operat-

ing quaint machines for chopping up these herbs. A large knife manipulated by a lever accomplishes the trick. Powdered skeletons of seahorses and other strange husks of sea life sometimes get exhibited in the shallow windows. On occasion, a cluster of virgin deer horns with the fuzz of youth still on them revive in old men the hope of recaptured vigor. A small amount of this remedy ground fine boasts a reputation for working wonders.

Offices of importing houses retain a fine dignity to their attractive interiors. Glass cases built against the walls hold display samples. What would be a prosaic accumulation of merchandise—the Chinese being masters of arrangement—becomes a thing of enchanting composition. At night, these offices, often retail shops, could be inhabited by grave gentlemen sitting primly in teakwood chairs set against the walls. This is visiting time. Often a domino game could be in progress, or the visitors will take a hand at mahjong, or cards, painted upon slender sticks.

Their genius for arrangement and color filters down even to the humblest levels. Keepers of sidewalk fruit stalls pile their mandarin oranges and grapefruit with unerring artistry; poultry dealers range their baskets of live fowl with balanced precision; and the fish markets, in spite of the handicap of updated white tiled counters, accomplish beautiful compositions by what seems to be a most casual arrangement of cod, flounder, and smelt.

It's factual reality: such singular sights are *foreign* to the rest of the city—except in *New Chinatown*, of course, within the inner Richmond district—whether you admit it or not, whether you like it or not. Look and *see*—and such wrongly denigrated concepts as *exotic* and *Oriental* could take on a whole new meaning and significance.

§

Tin How Temple
125 Waverly Place
Chinatown

Chief of the Chinese goddesses of course is *Tin How*, the Chinese Queen of Heaven. In her honor is that most impressive temple in *Waverly Place*—over the entrance of which is inscribed these words that have been an admonition from every revealer of God since the world began:

Purify thyself by fasting and self–denial.

On the floor below the **Temple of Tin How** are located the lodge rooms of the *Sue Sing(Hing)Benevolent Association*.

Decorations in the Joss House are a curious mixture of beauty and tawdriness: magnificent embroidered banners; golden silk flags; brass spears in symbolic design; walls of marble; furniture of ebony inlaid with mother–of–pearl; costly carvings splashed with gold–leaf; bronze incense bowls hundreds of years old mingled with paper decorations, battered kitchen chairs and saw–dust floors. In every Joss House is a bell to rouse the gods, sleeping or inattentive. Many of the lovely embroideries draping the walls are thanks offerings from grateful worshipers.

Peacock features, symbols of wisdom, are always used extensively in Joss House decoration. So, too, are five–toed dragon embroideries of the protecting deity of the Emperor. He has scales like any self–respecting dragon but instead of ears he sports two horns through which he hears. That five–toed dragon once guarded the sacred person of the Emperor, the Son of Heaven. But the dragon, generally speaking, is the guardian of the *rains*. He can release or withhold them at will.

§

FRANCESCO FERRARI
EXPLORES CHINATOWN

Early one evening I went to climb up four flights to the Joss House. All Joss Houses, as Rachel told me, hold forth on the topmost floor of any building which harbors them to be as near Heaven as possible.

Its enchanting interior charmed and delighted me on the side of taste and beauty. In spite of the gilt and barbaric color, this Temple to **Tin How**, the Goddess of Heaven, possesses a certain chaste beauty. She, who also rules the Seven Seas, is the same goddess, **Mazu**, who sat before the original altar raised to her in the gold rush days. That printed history of this Joss House fixes her advent in California as the year 1844 when a temple was raised to her by one, *Day Ju*, a Chinese pioneer.

Sharing honors with **Tin How** is the smooth–shaven Man–Dii, God of Literature, and the bearded Moi–Dii, God of the Military. Then there is Yan–Tan, the God of Justice. He rules over a supreme court that deals summarily with devils.

To the left of **Tin How** stand the twelve goddesses of motherhood. *NiLung* they are called. Each one of those goddesses is the guardian angel of children born in the particular month over which she rules.

Ranged on either side of the main altar are eight wands or spears. You see these in most Joss Houses. They are symbolic of eight holy people—seven men and one woman—who devised a plan to ward off devils by the simple expedient of being good. Their plan failing, they became, or were turned into fairies and given wands—as a more practical method of dealing with evil spirits.

There's a singularly beautiful carved arch through which you glimpse the main altar. It's intricately carved into a scene depicting the life of Confucius. Before the door of the old philosopher's house are two dragons, symbols of his power. That altar contains some fine pewter pieces set with enamel and precious stones. Those incense jars are crowned with Buddha lions.

Choi–Sun, the Goddess of Finance, has a shrine here. She rules the household and conserves money. She's the personification of the prudent wife, so esteemed in China. If you burn a joss stick to her, you do no more than reverence the perfect help mate. Fixing our minds on an ideal is the primary virtue in prayer. To reverence Choi–Sun is merely giving the idea of prudence its just due.

There is also a font of holy water in this Joss House to **Tin How** with an inscription admonishing visitors as they dip their fingers into its sacred depths to *"cleanse mind, heart and body before worshiping."* In evidence is the drum and gong to wake the gods as well as a fireplace in which prayers are burned. In the anteroom are strips of red paper lining the walls giving the names of contributors to the fund for maintaining the Joss House.

Offerings of paper money are purchased from the priest and prayers can be bought for a consideration. These are burned in little furnaces near the shrines. In some Joss Houses, it's said, you can buy prayers written by the priests that can be placed before the god in a little contraption like a music box which winds and unwinds the prayer over any given period of time.

If there are prayers for the benign gods, there are likewise curses for the devils. You buy these curses from the priest written in red ink upon yellow strips of paper. These are burned in a porcelain container and stirred into a cup of water. Then the priest, filling his mouth with the water and ashes, stamps about with a trident in one hand, spouting out the water and calling on the devils to begone!

There's a sacred ritual to seeking a god's help that goes something like this:

You enter and buy candles and incense from the priest in charge. Then you come into the presence of the divinity, clasp your hands and make a low bow. Next, you light your candles and incense, and kneeling on the mat before the god you call him by name three times.

Now's the moment to discover whether or not the god is in a receptive mood to hear your petition. You take two semi—oval pieces of wood, bow to the god again and toss those into the air. If both pieces of wood fall in the same position, it's a sign that the god is not disposed to listen. If one falls with the oval side down and the other with the flat side down, it's a good sign—the god's ear is inclined toward you.

Having determined this, you next take a bamboo cylinder filled with sticks, shaking them before the god until one falls to the floor. These are called *sticks of fate*. They're numbered and the priest, by consulting his book, gives you the answer to your petition.

§

Of course, I'd prayed to the God of Medicine, *Wah—Tah*, for Rachel's soundness and health—just as she'd once done for me. Whether my prayer was favorably received, I may never know, but I swore to myself that I'd try somehow to find out.

Given the transient mortality of this sometimes hellish existence we're all cursed and forced to live, once you suddenly lose the one and only one you love—whom you can no longer cherish and adore—what the hell's it matter in the end whether she was called *exotic*, *Oriental*, or *Chinese*? She was the girl—yes, *girl*—I truly and dearly and deeply loved. Then she was gone and I was lost—again.

All I could do I'd already done before: I dropped down, heartbroken, and bitterly wept.

FRANCESCO FERRARI
EXPLORES CHINATOWN

OTHER BOOKS BY JOSEPH COVINO JR
FICTION:

Francesco Ferrari Mines The Mission, A Homage To Vertigo

Francesco Ferrari Combs North Beach

Francesco Ferrari Navigates Fisherman's Wharf

San Francisco's Finest: Gunning For The Zodiac

Edgar Allan Poe's San Francisco: Terror Tales of the City

Frankenstein Resurrected

Arabian Nights Lost: Celestial Verses I

Arabian Nights Lost: Celestial Verses II

NONFICTION:

...And War For All: The Pledge of Subjection

...And Peace For All: The Pledge of Survival

Berkeley Bashed: Victim's Guide to the Backward, Barbaric, Butt–Ugly Bog

Elenore Sylvie Jeanne: My French Cookie

Impotent Cops: And Their Wee Willy Complex

Lab Animal Abuse: Vivisection Exposed!

Sexcapades by the Decades: The Twenties

Sexcapades by the Decades: The Thirties

Stay Fit(And Hot)For Life

UWF: University of West(Worst)Florida Exposed!

Yet Another Way The Federal Government Loots Its Citizens

203